A HOMELAND &
A HOMELAND

A HOMELAND &
A HOMELAND

Nabil Abu Shreikh

AuthorHouse™ LLC
1663 Liberty Drive
Bloomington, IN 47403
www.authorhouse.com
Phone: 1-800-839-8640

Published by AuthorHouse 05/06/2014

ISBN: 978-1-4969-0924-4 (sc)
ISBN: 978-1-4969-0922-0 (e)

Contents

To my Parents with love!

Acknowledgement

Thanks are due to my wife, my sons' mother, for her invaluable and patient help with typing and revising this book. She always sacrifices her leisure to lend me a hand. She's capable of the greatest love and reverence.

Nabil.

Introduction

Perfect happiness! Is it possible or is it only just a-will-o'-the wisp?

Some people find happiness in money and so their aim in life is to get money and more money with all possible means even though they are fabulously wealthy. Nevertheless, some of them are powerful with degrees and they occupy the highest administrative, social, political, economic or military positions in their communities. Soon, they generally find out they suffer inferiority complex of one thing or another; they feel jealous or even envious of some other people. Anyway, satisfied wealthy people with degrees, honor, decency, fame and respect are everywhere in our world.

Let's ask those powerful and wealthy people whether they are permanently and perfectly happy. Are their dreams always rosy or they are sometimes horrible nightmares? Sometimes, we all feel happy regardless of our state; patients or healthy, old or young, haves or have-nots and hungry or satisfied. We all have dreams and nightmares. We all smile and frown, cry and laugh but we all don't have the same amount of money, the same honesty, faithfulness, power, position or degree.

Unbelievably and shockingly some people find happiness in killing others or causing harm to others, but some others find happiness in rescuing lives of human beings even though they are their enemies. Millions of innocent people are killed in wars between countries or in civil wars. Why do all those wars break out? Who are the losers and who are the winners in the long run?

In the eighteen-sixties when the civil war broke out in the United States, the South and the North were losers but the whole U.S.A was the winner when the war stopped and forever. All Europe suffered in the Second Great War, but all Europe was the winner when the war ended and the European Union (EU) came to existence. It took the Europeans years of debating to reach an agreement to have their union, although gradually, see the light. Had they spent the same time debating to prevent the Second Great War from breaking out, Europe would have been wealthier, healthier and more developed and the EU would have been existed earlier. They would have saved millions of lives and billions or even trillions of dollars to build their universities, hospitals, industries, research centers, and to improve all features of life in Europe. Brainy people with talents are always available but they aren't always given the chance.

Others may debate that it was impossible to avoid that Great War; as well as many other civil or dual wars, because not all the warring factions were democratic states! Then it is the global democracy! It is that romantic word which had been degraded, ignored and denied in so many countries alongside the modern history. Perfect, real and genuine democracy is as important to people as air, water and food. It is just like any living thing. It can be lame, cross-eyed, blind, crippled, handicapped or paralyzed. It can be missing completely.

Nevertheless, all those who adopt any kind of democracy allege theirs is the most suitable one for their country and for their people. Some sectarian, military, tribal and dictatorial leadership have Parliaments or National Assemblies with uncontested election. They give the right to A and B to get governmental positions, especially senior officials and decision makers, to vote and to be candidates. At the same time they deny that right to C and D only because they are in the opposition or on sectarian, tribal, regional or racial grounds, regardless of their qualifications or loyalty to their country. One doesn't need to say those representatives in those parliaments aren't more than puppets controlled by the powerful rulers who hold those so-called parliaments as a kind of eye-wash; a kind of propaganda only. Nevertheless they give themselves the prerogative to dissolve those parliaments the time they like. Consequently, an uprising becomes a reasonable and inevitable product; sooner or later.

Civilized and democratic regions or nations unite and separate amiably and peacefully and they keep their friendly relations. Undemocratic governments are always against their peoples and against their neighbors' aspirations for unreasonable grounds. Tens of civil or dual wars which followed the Second Great War in the last seventy years were completely in or between undemocratic countries of ruthless leaderships or at least one of the two warring factions was undemocratic. Not a civil war took place in a democratic country nor a war broke out between two democratic countries. Most of those countries which witnessed those wars were neither rich nor powerful. Most of them were poor with rare natural resources and weak industry. In general, their infrastructure and their vital services like drainage, health, education, security, transportation, communication, water and power supplies were so poor. Corruption, unemployment, ignorance, poverty, inflation and diseases reigned. Consequently, educated and enlightened people in those countries flee the insecure and unsafe environment; the tyrant and ruthless dictatorial regimes; the police states. Those people who desert their countries, mostly to the neighboring or to the democratic and wealthy states seeking wealth, security and safety find themselves, in many cases, struggling within armed opposition, inside and outside their homeland, against their brutal leadership. Finally, a civil or a dual war between neighbors breaks out or at least clashes with all kinds of arms take place. Although the dictators of those countries exclaim they are unable to afford to build more schools or to develop hospitals, they make and import tanks, missiles, mines, air fighters and bombers and heavy weapons to war against their neighbors or even against their people. They build prisons and train ill-bred and hard-hearted men to oversee the prisoners, mostly politicians, whose accusation is always opposition which is interpreted into conspiracy against the ruling group—if those prisoners aren't executed before or in the first few days of their imprisonment. Nevertheless, those dictators deposit millions or even billions in foreign banks.

Let me close this introduction, although long, with this short story which is a fact.

It is well known that prisons or jails all over the world only accept offenders and suspects because they caused harm to society, but we all know that not every prisoner is an offender or a suspect.

A prison inspector visited one of the infamous prisons in one of the police states. To his amazement, the prison population was two hundred and fifty-seven but the record shows two hundred and fifty-six only. The prison manager gathered the inmates and they stood in lines in the prison yard. As every inmate had been known by a number, not by their names, he ordered aloud, "Number two hundred and fifty-seven, raise up your hand!" Not a hand was lifted. Then he asked, "Who hasn't got a number?" One of them heaved a sigh of relief and raised his hand. Later, the inspector together with the prison officers found that one of the prison officers had asked his guest who was visiting him in his office to excuse him for five minutes and went out of the room. The guest stayed for hours in that officer's room but his host didn't come back. In the evening, the sweeper came to clean the room. When he found that man in the officer's room, he said he was not allowed to stay there alone and so he sent him to wait for his host in the secretary's room where he spent the night.

When the secretary came in the next morning, he was surprised to find the man in his room and so he had to tell the officer in charge. Finally, that ill-fated visitor found himself sharing the prisoners their cells for six years.

Then the inspector said to the guest-inmate that he didn't think he had booked into a hotel. He had to pay for accommodation, services and amenities of the past six years or he'd be imprisoned for another six. When the guest-prisoner asked him to call his wife, a friend or a relative, the inspector refused and said it was a military zone and he had to paddle his own canoe by himself. Then he turned to the prison manager and told him to give that man a dead prisoner's number!

By the way, that country has its own parliament but human rights and all liberties were not allowed to enter it decades ago.

The truth isn't always very palatable! It's sometimes stranger than fiction!

I

Afasinamea is a country in the Eastern hemisphere. It came to existence when two neighboring nations, although different in culture, united and formed a democratic federal state more than half a century ago. It was supposed the two cultures had to interpenetrate each other to become virtually a single and unique one in the long run; during the unity time, like all the federal states in the world which adopted the global democracy. Later, selfishness and personal, tribal and sectarian interests contradicted such interpenetration.

Together with the growth of nationalism, injustice, unemployment, inflation, corruption and the foreign intervention, they took the decision to separate optionally, amiably and peacefully. Two new democratic states; West Afasinamea and East Afasinamea re-emerged to existence. The boundary inhabitants between the two countries were mostly the issue of mixed marriages from both countries.

Hungupville is a fair-sized town in West Afasinamea counting about a hundred thousand inhabitants. It was situated on two hills, a few miles from the boundary line between the two Afasinameas. It is mostly surrounded with woodlands of giant olive, oak, pine, carob, acacia and cedar trees. Between the edge of the woods and the town, there are vine yards and orchards with thick fruitful trees like citrus, apple, apricot, cherry, fig, pear, plum, to name just a few fruitful trees. Wherever one goes inside the town or in the suburbs, one will be amazed of the green with patches of uncountable colored roses and flowers. For these flowers and roses, especially in spring and in summer, the town had better been called Scentville, Flowerville or Coloredville!

There are some streams and gullies crossing the town from the north to the south. Five years ago, Lord Mayor imported six thousand little fishes of different kinds and let them free in the small lake where most of the gullies and streams meet. With time passage, the number of those fishes increased amazingly; many folds. Some of those fishes became very large. Recently, only Hungupvillians are allowed to catch Hungupvillian fishes for amusement only.

For the abundant flowers, roses and fruitful trees, honey-bees found Hungupville woods, farms, gardens and orchards suitable and secure places to build their hives in. Hungupvillian bee-honey is the most delicious in the whole area. Birds of all sizes and species build their nests everywhere on and around those two hills. They remarkably increased in number. Catching or hunting birds in Hungupville is law breaking.

Those two hills are mostly covered with dew and haze in the spring as well as in the summer mornings. They keep flowers, vegetable plants and fruits unsullied up to the middle of the fall season. Summer white clouds form a natural parasol protecting the white houses and the gardens from the scorching sunrays in the afternoons. The green and the wet breeze stimulate Hungupvillian youths; males and females, to walk along the drives or across the woods with their never-ending smiles and their linked arms late in the afternoon. They also stimulate their parents and their grandpas to walk to the public parks and to enjoy the scenic views.

Hungupville hospital was established fifteen years ago and its university; The Applied Sciences University of Hungupville, opened its doors for the first time twelve years ago. Most of its students generally came from other cities. Those students had never got the chance to be placed or to be employed full time or part time in Hungupville. The answer was always 'No Vacancies!'

For leisure and amusement, aside from sports facilities, all other attractions like night life, amusement centers . . . were missing.

Its canning and converting industries put Hungupville in the class of the most economically advanced towns in the country. Its inhabitants complained of the forty-hour work a week, in addition to the compulsory nine-hour overtime work, paid for and tax free. The surrounding towns, especially those which were behind the boundary line in the East, suffered unemployment. Therefore, they envied Hungupville its egoism. Meantime, Hunupville inhabitants envied them their free time. For housing, shopping, farming, manufacturing, and engineering products, Hungupville was self-sufficient.

Politically, West Afasinamea chose to be a neutral country. They adopted the policy of nonintervention and their democracy was an archetype for other countries. Racial or excessive parties were not allowed to take part in the daily policies of the country. To criticize any other country, its leaders or its institutions was illegal. Nevertheless, some other countries' leaders looked at West Afasinamea as an easy prey. Its natural resources, its strong economy and its peaceful policy enticed them to invade or annex it more than once.

II

At separation and without a war or no-mercy corruption, the East struggled against an underdeveloped economy. Later disruptions sprung from coups and frequent periods of drought dealt severe blows to the agricultural sector, once prosperous. As the undeclared and nonstop war between the East and the West took place in the junta time, it further drained their economy. Consequently, the Easterners expelled more than half a million people of Western origin to the West. The East had to rely heavily on aid from multilateral agencies to sustain its economy. Financial resources announced that as a consequence of East Afasinamea's failure to implement significant reforms, they'd reduce financial aid. Therefore, more than half of the population lived in poverty.

Mr. Martin Miese was one of those who were drafted into the Information Corps in the army when he was newly graduated from college. His country, friendly to all neighbors and peaceful, was threatened by the neighboring dictator of East Afasinamea who had been in power after a successful coup since two years. He had ambitions to annex it to his country by force although the two nations were different in culture and regime. And so the draft was imposed in West Afasinamea. Its leaders were right in their expectations. Their neighbors didn't wait long to attack them. They crushed the defensive line and crossed the boundary. Although with Pyrrhic victory, the invaders advanced killing and plundering as they went deep inland.

Then the West uncompromising, underground and armed resistance came into sight with unbreakable spirit of the defenders to push the invaders out of their country. In a separate event, three soldiers of their enemies were ambushed and two of them were killed. The third was seriously wounded. He could hardly crawl and get a hide in a shady nook in the woods, behind a rock. A West Afasinamean soldier, Martin Miese, used to spend some time every day in the very place contemplating war and fighting. When he got there, he was surprised to find the wounded soldier occupying his place. Martin aimed his rifle at him and ordered him to lift his hands up. The wounded soldier couldn't move that he was in a state near the death. He could hardly say, "Kill me, please!" Mr. Miese walked cautiously and slowly towards him, "How come you're here?" But the wounded soldier was too weak to move or say any more word; he had got four bullets in his pelvis. And so Martin put his rifle aside and asked him what his name was when he was helping him to lie down on his back and plunging his hand into his first-aid bag. "G o d f r e y." The wounded soldier said with difficulty. Martin made him drink and asked him to take his pants off but Godfrey neither said nor did anything. Martin, "I gonna help you. Take'em off!" But that was in vain. So, Martin pulled Godfrey's pants down when he was plucking some pads, a vessel of antiseptic and a bandage from his bag. He cleaned the clotted blood around the wounds, poured antiseptic on them and covered them with all the pads he had together with the bandage. "Can you walk?" Martin asked him. The wounded soldier was too weak to say any word; he fainted right off. And so Martin carried him on his back and walked to the highway which was around a hundred yards from them. He had to step over more than one putrefying corpse on his way to the highway which the invaders; the Easterners, would certainly drive along.

It was hard to say whether Mr. Miese and Godfrey were lucky or unlucky! When they were at the side of the street, a patrol in a jeep stopped opposite to them. Mr. Miese gave a sign to the soldiers to calm down telling them he was unarmed and they could take him a prisoner. Later, he was accused of shooting Godfrey and taking him a prisoner although what he wanted was to save the wounded-soldier's life. He was bleeding badly. A helicopter was called and took Godfrey. The other soldier; the rescuer, was tied to the front of the jeep.

Martin Miese was shocked to see all those dead men at the two sides of the road. The bodies of the victims weren't a pretty sight. Hundreds of corpses of military and nonmilitary of both warring factions were lying under the trees, between rocks at the two sides of the road. As the highway was mostly covered with debris since the two warring factions bombed tanks, armored cars, all kinds of vehicles and beautiful buildings which were reduced to ruins and tons of different shells filled the road in addition to the fallen trees, the jeep was zigzagging and running slowly.

There was an old woman at the right side of the road hugging a corpse which was headless and armless. She was moaning and wailing. A young man was standing by her trying to convince her that her husband was a civilian while the corpse she was hugging was of a military one. A few yards away, there was a couple turning killed children and looking at their burnt or deformed faces. They were searching for their child who was in the school when it was bombed to ruins. Two young girls on the left were contemplating a corpse. The officer in the jeep held the driver's shoulder and ordered aloud, "Stop!" Then he turned his head towards the two girls and said, "What're you doing here? It's a military zone. You shouldn't be here!" One of the girls shouted while crying, "I search for my boyfriend. He was a civilian; unarmed. Why did you kill him?" Then he turned to the other girl who was crying, too, and inquired, "And you?" The girl said sobbing, "He's my brother." Then the officer to the driver, "Move!"

When the jeep arrived at the first military station, they took Martin as a POW to be investigated. Nevertheless, he looked very pleased that he was smiling. When the officer asked him why he was smiling although he was a prisoner of war, he said, "For two reasons. The first was that soldiers had to fight and kill, but I neither fought nor killed anyone! The second was that I was in danger when I had my fire arm but now I feel safe and happy as I rescued the so-called enemy soldier, Godfrey."

"What's your name?" The officer asked him. "Martin Miese, Sir." The prisoner said. Then the officer asked amazed. "Did you shoot Godfrey or did you rescue him?" The prisoner's face shown up with pleasure and said, "Did he survive?" The investigator nodded and left the room.

An hour later, he returned to the room and asked, "Why did you rescue Godfrey although he's an aggressor and an invader? Don't you call us aggressors and invaders?" Martin Miese answered, "Because your politicians, like ours, spend billions to have their sons and their brothers killed in battlefields. Is this war fair and convincing? Is it your own option and your own will to take part in this war or you were ordered only to go to the war regardless of your own will? Have you got a family?" The investigator nodded. "If you were killed, who would be the victim? You? Your widow? Your orphans? Your siblings? Your friends and relatives? All of you are victims; all of us. You can't say accurately how many of your people are affected by war. Can't the politicians, the decision makers, meet and reach an agreement? They would have done much to save our lives if they wished. Although I'm a prisoner and unarmed I feel happy. I have never killed any man, but I could rescue a life. Some people boast about the number of people they killed, the air fighters they downed and the tanks or the vehicles with their men they bombed. Do you feel happy and you're a conqueror, free and heavily armed?" The investigator stroke the table with his hand and ordered, "Shut up! You're here to answer; not to ask."

In fact, the investigator was amazed. The prisoner's words were touching, convincing and simple. Then he asked, "Tell me please. Are you a graduate?" "Yes Sir, I am. I was going to be granted my MA when the war broke out." The prisoner answered. "Specialization?" "Sociology, Sir!" "Why did you choose Sociology?" "To recognize that Christians as well as Non-Christians, military and nonmilitary, love life and hate war." Martin Miese answered. Then the investigator asked, "If I let you free, what will you do?" "I'll go back to my job; to my store." Mr. Miese answered. "You won't participate in any war, will you?" The investigator asked. "I wish you asked me to protest against war; to call for peace; to lift a placard with 'No More Wars! Peace Now and Forever!' The rich finance wars! We're the price; our families are the price! Well, if I killed Godfrey; if you killed me, if we killed each other, aside from politicians, war veterans, investors and financiers, who will be the winner? No one for sure. May I ask a question?" The investigator roared with laughter and said, "Haven't you asked any questions yet? Go ahead!" "Do you like warring, killing, bombing and destruction?" Martin Miese asked. With a smile that didn't suggest any kind of pleasure on the officer's face, he looked at the ceiling thoughtful but he said nothing.

It was six pm when the officer made a phone call. A womanly voice answered, "Medical Corps. This is Dr. Myra. Can I help you?" "This is Cap Simon Limonnes from IGA; Intelligence-Gathering Agency. Today's losses, please!" "Just a moment, Cap Simon. Err . . . one hundred and thirty-one losses in lives, one hundred and fifty-two wounded; many of them are in critical conditions and they're in the emergency room now." "Are those casualties of today only?" Cap Simon inquired. "Unfortunately yes, Captain; of today only." Dr. Myra answered. "Dr. Myra, when you face the press, the losses in lives are three; only three and the wounded are, err . . . twelve. Thank you, Doctor." He hung up and rose up to leave the room when his mobile-phone rang. "Captain Simon Limonnes from the IGA." "Simon, Mom's seriously ill. The doctor says we've to put her on the kidney machine." His sister Sabrina said. "Oh, Sabrina, take her to the hospital and put her on the machine." Cap Simon said. "But we're in the hospital at the moment, Simon. They said they'd closed

the Kidney Section. We need to take her to the capital."
"Ok, I'll be there by you in half an hour. Bye, bye" Captain
Simon Limonnes said and reached to the door to leave the
room. The prisoner looked at him from the corner of his eye
and an ironic smile was drawn on his face.

Three months passed. Neither the conquerors were able
to control the caught territory or attain any of their goals,
nor was the obstinate resistance able to push them out of
their country. It was seriously risky for the conquerors to
withdraw their troops from the caught territory.

When the financiers and the investors closed their
money faucets and the two factions were tired of war, both
of them sought mediators to solve the problem of war and
fighting between them.

Another five months passed after the Security-Council
Seize-Fire Resolution including two months of indirect
negotiations; a UN delegate had to act as an intermediary
between the two warring factions, then direct negotiations
and finally the warring factions were able to exchange
prisoners of war and the troops returned behind the approved
boundary line between the two countries.

When food aid was badly needed and with some
politicians' support, the investors and the financiers' role
emerged again. The two countries had to reconstruct their
destroyed infrastructure, factories, buildings, means of
transportation and of course their arms! That would cost
billions and billions of dollars but they had to close some
universities and some scientific research centers. The jobless,
sufferers of sordid poverty, and all those who depended upon
the National Welfare to survive had to face their fate by
themselves. The war ate away all funds.

Captain Simon Limonnes, the investigator, thought long of corruption, war, fighting, losses in lives, destruction and of democracy. All the leadership including the dictator of East Afasinamea was to blame. Such leadership gang was mainly of one tribe and they didn't come to office by elections, and so they wouldn't leave office by elections. Their term was for long. So, Cap Simon and other officers from all regions of East Afasinamea planned to revolt against the dictatorial leadership and to establish a democratic government. As the IGA had put tails on some suspected officers to check their movement and by the infamous telephone-patting affair, their plan was uncovered and of course it failed. Some of them were executed; they faced a firing squad without trial or court martial. Some others were imprisoned and a few were lucky to flee their country. Cap Limonnes was one of those who fled their country and crossed the boundary line seeking shelter abroad to survive.

As West Afasinamea was in a stringent economic situation, Mr. Limonnes didn't like to stay there. In one week only, he was able to immigrate to Nectarland. Even there; in Nectarland, he declined to be a political refugee. He planned to be an ordinary naturalized Nectarlandic citizen and to depend upon himself in his new homeland.

Five years later, the leadership in East Afasinamea was removed by armed insurrection and democracy was re-established. Simon disliked turning back to his mother land. He liked the new life style in Nectarland; his new homeland.

One day, when Mr. Limonnes was watching TV, there was a commercial. A housing company is advertising luxurious apartments and villas for average prices in New East Afasinamea Suburb, north west of Nectarland capital.

Interested people could call an assigned phone number. Mr. Limmones phoned them up and asked about the company's owners. They were some of the previous junta members of East Afasinamea! He shook his head amazed and wondered, "Where have they got the work capital from?"

III

Martin Miese returned to his country to find his regiment disbanded. He went back to his store to make butter and cheese from cow and sheep milk. His business was successful and it was developing. He married Sofia Farms and had a son called Joseph. When Martin was thirty-three, he received a letter from the army in Monday morning. As a reservist, he had to be in his newly-formed regiment at the seashore, north to the capital before Wednesday noon.

His son Joseph; nine years old then, returned from his school to the store in the afternoon. He always helped his father cleaning the store and keeping things in order. Then they closed the store and walked home together at sunset. That afternoon when Joseph entered the store, Martin burst into tears. "Are you crying, Dad? Is it the backache again?" Joseph asked and hugged his father who was sitting on a small wooden chair. Martin couldn't control himself. He hugged his son, kissed his forehead and said, "Ok, Joe. Let's go home." "So early, Dad?"

Martin put the butter, cheese and milk he had in the giant fridge and Joseph cleaned the store. Then Martin closed it, grabbed his son's hand and went home. He didn't stop crying all the way long.

His wife was stunned when she saw him sad and his eyes blood red. "What's the matter, Martin? Is it the backache again?" She asked him worried. Martin cried glumly. In a chocked voice he told her that he had received a letter from the army. "Reserves! Right?" She asked. He nodded and fell down in a seat behind him. "Umm, Err, is the war breaking out? Against whom? We don't have enemies. Our neighbors are good countries and our government policies are moderate. It must be a mistake of an incompetent mad officer." She said angrily. "Our super powerful allies will build an air base on the Northern Mountain." Martin said. "Why? Isn't there a place in their countries to build their air bases on? We seek peace; not war! Martin, I can't understand the relationship between the new air base and calling the reservist troops. And tell me please, can we start an air base of our own in their countries?" Sofia, Martin's wife asked infuriated. "Yes, we can. The Prime Minister declared in the morning that we could build air and marine bases on their lands and they would leave whenever we asked them to. Although they are a defensive force, they had to defend us by defending themselves. Nevertheless, they aren't going to take share in our war against any aggressors, but they would support us logistically. Over and above, they paid for the land which was rented to build the base on and there would be more than twenty new jobs available for our jobless people. It's military cooperation. Our super powerful friends are going to war against a country with a dictatorial leadership and aggressive intents in a troubled and hot area. They seek our country and our men to help them achieve their goals." Martin said. "Super Powers seek help from our men! What do other countries seek? Certainly, our girls!" Sofia said disdainfully. In spite of Martin's feeling of bitterness, he burst with laughter. Joe was listening to his parent's conversation. He was very pleased to see his father laugh.

With a jerk from his head, Martin indicated that Sofia had to follow him to the bedroom. "Listen, Sofia." He started. "I'm leaving tomorrow. Joseph's literate. He'd better be removed from school so as to help you in the store." Sofia nodded thoughtful. Then she said, "But he's still a little kid." Martin gave her a side look of annoyance but he said nothing.

As Joseph was only nine years old, Sofia didn't incline to remove him from school. She worked in the store alone suffering from rheumatism. Her back and her knees ached unbearably. After three years, Joe's removal from school was inevitable when his father was killed in a plane crash. She made him work in the store and she was overseeing and directing him, unable to do any hard work.

Joseph used to open the store early in the morning and to close it at dusk. At seven-thirty every morning, he stood leaning on his elbow at the store door, watching his classmates going to school with their bags in their hands, under their arms or on their backs. They exchanged smiles with him or they sometimes exchanged the morning greeting. He was jealous of them. They, too, had the same feeling. He was a man in their eyes, but they had a flourishing and secure future in his. Sometimes, he cried.

When his mother died, Joseph was left alone. He was saddled with heavy tasks and he had to shift for himself. He became more concerned in his store that he worked hard from sunrise to sunset alone. The milk truck used to unload thirty-five gallons of cow milk and twenty gallons of sheep milk. That was the Miese's share. Then seventy and thirty, only a few weeks before his mother died. At last, the whole truck loading five hundred gallons of cow milk and two hundred gallons of sheep milk was unloaded at Miese's store which was developed from manual labor to an automatic small manufactory, to the largest one, to the only butter, cheese and cream factory in Hungupville. Recently, a second flavored-cream line was added. Finally, Mr. Miese became the king of butter, cheese and cream industry in the whole area. Miese's products were so famous that when the market for butter, cheese and cream was saturated, his products found a ready sale. They had never been undersold nor had he needed to undercut the price. He sacrificed his health and his comfort to money making in the salad days, as he used to call those years; his late adolescence and early twenties. His mother passed away when he was twenty-one.

When he got married, he was twenty-six years old. He bought a villa in a straight and well-paved boulevard lined with trees and regular one-colored villas at the two sides. His villa included back and front gardens. The trees in both gardens screened the villa from public view. Although it consisted of two stories only, there was an electric escalator and a set of wide and safe stairs. Those stairs were surfaced with a thick layer of cork. The walls were heavily ornate with different and expressive pictures and paintings of the most famous and modern painters. They were mostly salacious. One of the old men, a visitor, once commented, "Oh! What have you left to the devil?" Nonetheless, he admired those paintings that he stood many minutes gazing at them. There were also clocks of different sizes, designs and makes, different statues, vases, samplers and other articles of all kinds made of ivory, gold, silver, copper, bronze or china on shelves and on stands in the study and in the sitting room. There were hundreds of books, which Joseph had never read, covered with dust on shelves in the study which had two large windows looking at the back garden. One could sit on a rocking chair and enjoy reading a book or a newspaper while listening to the birds singing in the trees. There was also a modern PC on a desk and a comfortable seat opposite to it. Next to the study, there was a large room or a hall which could seat fifty people or more. The floor was completely surfaced with thick silky carpets. The doors and the windows of the villa were all screened against mosquitoes, flies or any other kind of insects. Joseph's car which he bought when his first son Matt came to life was of the last model and of the most expensive make. Joseph Miese was fabulously rich and his villa looked to the visitor for the first time a gallery or a museum. Nevertheless, he always complained that he had everything one might aspire, but only one thing he missed; a university degree which could not be bought. Factually, he wished it could be!

Twenty years ago, Joseph got married. Gillian Showne, his wife, was twenty-four when he married her. She was healthy, blond, tall and rather slim with soft skin, broad shoulders, short fair hair and blue eyes. Joe always dreamed of a blue-eyed woman and luckily he got a very beautiful woman with so dark blue eyes in addition to a kind of sweet music in her voice.

Gillian was a farmer's daughter who was removed from school when she was fourteen. Mr. Showne; her father, wasn't interested in the physical or mental education of his daughter. He removed her from school when the Department of Education took the decision to close her school and to move the girls to another one, one mile away from their home. He wanted her to look after the house when his wife and he where on their farm most of the time. The evacuees, whose houses were destroyed in the front zone, got the opportunity and took the deserted school a shelter.

The Shownes used to go to the farm in the early morning and they returned home late in the afternoon. Sometimes, they returned at night but they rarely slept in the farm-house. Gillian grew up and she was twenty-two. She was alone depending upon herself every day, most of the year and so she felt lonely. Unless the Shownes had a TV with hundreds of channels, Gillian couldn't bear that loneliness.

Joseph, twenty-four years old then; two years older than Gillian, was tall, rather fat and stout. He had a dark moustache and dark eyes. He used to pass by her house twice a day; on his way to his store and back to his home. At the beginning, they looked at each other amusingly. Then they nodded and smiled. By and by, they exchanged a word. In the second week, they had a can of beer, a cup of coffee or a glass of tea and a biscuit in the lobby. And then, they moved from the lobby to the sitting room.

In the first few days, she had pants, jeans or a skirt going down below the knee and a long-sleeved shirt or a T-shirt. When they drew nearer to each other and went deeper inside the house, her clothes became shorter, thinner and more transparent. The skirt which was one foot below the knee became one foot over; a mini skirt. The pants became shorts and the jeans were so narrow. The long-sleeved shirt became short-sleeved, then sleeveless and finally it became a strapless top. Sometimes, she had a lacy maxi-dress with a deep V-collar that went down to the middle of her breast parting. She sat longer time opposite to her mirror and sprayed a little perfume behind her ears and at her breast parting and round.

One Saturday, when Gillian and Joseph were sitting side by side in the sitting room and he was talking and waving with his hand, it brushed gently against her breast by accident. He turned to her with an intent to apologize, but she shivered, closed her eyes and her heart beats could be heard. She was extremely thrilled. His touch electrified her heart. Joseph became quite demented although he was inexperienced in the field of love. Her eyes, lips, face, head, legs, arms, hands and fingers all gestured to Joe what to do without a word was spoken. It was a simple and easy lesson assigned to Grade One. His lips passed across her neck and her cheeks until their lips stuck together. He licked her mouth and his tongue slid within it. She shuddered and melted into his arms burning. Finally, he deflowered her. From then on, she addicted the morning-after pills.

On Monday, her face colored rosy and red. Her eyelashes became thicker, longer and darker and her eyebrows became thinner or rather they disappeared. Only a drawn black line replaced each eyebrow. Finally, Gillian and Joseph decided to spend the time; the whole time they stay together, in the bedroom. It was unacceptable to waste any more minutes anywhere else.

There; in the bedroom, they felt how heavy their clothes were and how happy they would be when they got rid of that heavy burden. Then, in ten to fifteen minutes, Gillian lay down on her bed panting; very tired. She closed her eyes and turned to the other side, satisfied. When Joe jumped down from the bed, and stood for seconds contemplating her, she turned again and lay on her back, licked her lips, smiled at Joe and closed her eyes again with satisfaction.

Generally, Gillian used to wake up at six sharp in the morning. She stayed in her bed counting the seconds and the minutes. Her parents left home at six-thirty. Time was slow. At six thirty-five, she left her bed, had a quick shower, dressed in her lightest and shortest clothing and consulted her mirror. Then she made coffee and milk and roasted a few pieces of bread in their broiler pan. There would be jam or honey, butter and roasted bread on the breakfast table. Joe came between seven and seven-five. It took them a quarter of an hour to have their coffee and their breakfast.

At first, he spent half an hour a day with Gillian. A few weeks before their wedding, they spent half of the day together in the bedroom. That relationship between Joe and Gill lasted two years.

Gillian proved to be a wonderful beloved sweetheart before the wedding and a magnificent housewife ever after. When Matthew, their son, came to life, she became an excellent mother.

The day he had a son, Joseph bought a new car. It was majestic, of the last model and a first-class make. Since his product of butter, cheese and cream increased, he had to move his store to a more spacious place. He absorbed then three truckloads of milk; two truckloads of cow milk and one truckload of sheep milk. He bought new machines and employed a staff of workers and employees with degrees, although he had already employed a few since years. The time he talked to his employees during tea or dinner breaks, he felt educated and happy. He would not hesitate to make his son Matthew drink book soup or inject him with book-ash solution if he were told that would affect him positively; his intelligence and his memory definitely, that he would have one of the great minds of the age. He wanted him to be genius in every trade and the unique scientist of his age; Marconi II!

IV

On his first day at school, Matt had to go by their own private car. It was safe with extra strength; safety belts, unbreakable windscreen and a body that was designed to stand up to crashes. The chauffeur had to wait at the school gate until he was sure that Matt was on his desk in his classroom. The school gatekeeper was paid only to ring Matt's father daily to remind him that the school would finish in a quarter of an hour. When Joseph appointed a safe man as manager, in addition to the staff he had previously employed, and they could manage his factory completely and successfully, he felt secure about the future of his industry. He was able to go home early that he arrived home simultaneously with his son Matt.

After a quick shower and dinner, he went into his bedroom, only with his underpants on, where his wife Gillian had preceded him. In addition to the breakfast, Joseph had a pound of cream and another pound of milk to check and to taste only. In short, he had two pounds of white protein in the morning. At dinner, he had another two pounds of red and green proteins. He had to walk or run one mile at least, in the early morning and another mile late in the afternoon or in the evening to digest and to sharpen his appetite. He always had a big supper with

23

desserts, fruit and a quart of beer. If he forgot to run one or even two miles a day, oxen would be jealous of his fatness. There would be a quarrel with Gillian any day his appetite wasn't sharp. Nevertheless, he always had surplus energy that he was virile.

Gillian hired a single female tutor to oversee Matt's study at home. She was twenty-three, and she was a graduate with a degree. She was medium-sized, with long auburn hair that hung down almost to her waist, hazel eyes and she was dressing in fashions. Her way of speaking was that of an educated woman. Matt went to her in the study, soon after dinner. She had to look after him doing his homework and reviewing the next-day periods. She arrived at the Miese's house a quarter of an hour after Matt and his father had arrived, crossed the back garden and then she got into the house from a side access and straight to the study where she checked Matt's timetable, prepared for the next day periods, checked and did the homework with him and corrected his mistakes. She also drew pictures or sketches on the smart board or on paper sheets and hung the wall pictures she had on the wall. Finally, she prepared games and toys to play with Matt and to amuse him. Her daily mission usually finished in three hours. Then she gave Matt 'a Good afternoon' at four forty-five and turned back home before sunset. During those three hours, she had her eyes open and her ears and her nostrils dilated. She always smelt that wonderful perfume and heard the bedroom and the bathroom doors squeaking as well as those soft words full of passion and ecstasies of love. She only sighed, put her tongue out and licked her lips. Sometimes, she bit the lower one.

One day, late in September, Gillian received a phone call from her mother telling her that her father, Albert Showne, had suddenly felt a sharp pain in his chest. He was hot with fever and he was sweating although he felt cold. Gillian rang the chauffeur who was waiting for Matt at the school gate and told him she was going with Matt to call at her parents' house and that the tutor didn't need to come on that day. He should call her.

The children rushed pell-mell down the stairs. They surged forward scrambling and pushing each other trying to get out of the school gate to buy an ice-cream or a chocolate before they got into their buses. The chauffeur was worried about Matt. He left the car and got into the school yard looking for him. There was a quarrel in the school yard. One of the pupils was lying on the ground bleeding. When he caught sight of Matt, he hurried and clasped him in his arm. They both got into the car and drove fast. The chauffeur asked Matt about that boy who was lying on the ground. Matt said he should have been trodden on when he fell down.

Gillian was waiting for them at the door of her house. She was worried about her father. Before the car had completely stopped, Gillian opened the passenger back door and got into the car. The chauffeur drove fast to her parents.

V

The tutor was punctual. She came in and sat in the study room, doing her task as usual. Joseph had been told that Gillian and Matt had gone to her parents' house and that the tutor wasn't coming. He had a shower and then he had his dinner alone. As Gillian wasn't at home, he didn't dash to the bedroom as usual. Instead, he headed to the study, only with his stretch cotton thong on to amuse himself on his PC; reading the news, some ads and some classifieds. The tutor was standing still in the study gazing at a marble statue on the shelf. She was lost in admiration when her eyes met with Joseph's. Both were surprised; none of them was expecting the other. He was at loss but she felt shy. She didn't find any word to say, but her eyes as well as her mouth opened wide. "What a sturdy man he is!" She said to herself. She turned to a chair and sat down. She looked nymphomaniac.

It took Joe a few seconds before he could find his tongue again. "I didn't know you were here." He initiated. "Matt's at his grandpa's together with Gill. Her father's ill. Didn't they call you?" He added and sat in the nearest thing that occurred to be; a chair recliner. "Really?" She asked amazed and smiled shyly. Her smile was so sweet. "None called me." She replied laconically, moving her hand to the upper button, below the collar's one, which was already undid. Her hand went to the third one and started undoing it so slowly when Joseph asked her, "What would you like to drink Miss . . . ?" She introduced herself, "Eleanor." And she smiled again. "Any cold drink to quench my thirst, please." She demanded. When he returned with a glass of water, her chiffon-satin open-cup bralette had strikingly pushed forward binding two smothered clumps in a sweet pomegranate-size each, struggling to get free and to breathe fresh air. The bra was light hazel, her eyes color. When Joseph was handing her the glass, he felt her hot breath and her sweet scent. He smiled maliciously. Then he backed two steps contemplating her and pointing at the two lower buttons then he asked, "Need help for those two?" She nodded and whispered sweetly, "Yes, please. Could you (miming)?"

Joe knew the importance of time. He wasn't the man who might lose a few seconds without doing something he liked. He not only undid the two buttons, but he helped her take off her shirt and wrapped his arms around her waist. She, too, was very interested in what was going on. She wrapped his neck with her arms and both kissed passionately. She felt she was in heaven when she was between his arms. They were burning when he carried her on his shoulder and moved out of the study. One of his hands was holding her legs and the other was brushing her back and a little lower gently. One of her hands was probing his back and the other was holding her shirt. Then she said cunningly but softly and gratifyingly, "Where're you takin' me?" Joseph knew she didn't mean to ask and so he didn't need to answer. Then she whispered delicately, "Put me down!" when she was punching his back gently. He headed to the bedroom saying, "I'll do, in the paradise!" "Wow!" That was her only comment.

He got into the bedroom and put her softly on the bed, bent over her and kissed. When he rose up, she felt she had to take her jeans off. Joe drew her to his chest and his fingers ran across her neck and across her back and unfastened her bra. Then his fingers disappeared in her hair but her arms were below his and her hands were holding his shoulder blades. Their tongues went into the other's mouth mutually licking, tasting and tickling one another. Then his hands were stripping her off the very little thing that remained on; namely her V-thong. He sat opposite to her on the bed contemplating her. And then she leaned her back against the pillows, closing her hazel eyes dreamful. He drew nearer and his fingers went probing her in a way she had never been touched before. In a moment, she opened her eyes and laughed pointing at his thong, "What about yours? Feel cold?" She said and went on laughing, although she was still shy! He said instantly, "Sorry, I can't! I've never done that. Gillian did. Could you . . ." He didn't finish his last phrase when she extended her hand quickly towards him and made him get rid of his thong. Both were busy. She was helping him to take his thong off and checking his hairy broad chest and his muscular arms and he was probing her soft, so sensitive and warm flesh. When she felt his fingers probing her soft flesh, his lips sucking her lower one, she was infatuated with him. She took the right position to have him got into her. She felt the utmost excitement as he was moving up and down inside her. To lift her pelvis up, she curved and drove him deeper in, feeling the pleasures of the seventh heaven.

Later, they were lying on the bed side by side. She was subconscious but he was quite lively although his heart was still hammering. He rolled on his side and kissed across her neck and nibbled at her earlobe. One of his fingers went down examining her nipples. On tracing little circles on and around them softly, they were so hard and moved up refreshed. They were longing for a lick, a suck or at least a little kiss. And then his fingers moved smoothly and gently down, down, to some other breathtaking spots of her naked body. "Oh, Eleanor! Have you ever been told you're the sweetest, the softest, the warmest, the sexiest and the most gratifying woman one has ever seen?" He asked passionately with his fingers, lips, and tongue still busy. "Oh! Oh, Joe! (she moved her head so slowly and settled it on his shoulder.) Have-you . . . (breathless and tired.) Oh, ever known— Oh—you're—the—strongest—the fiercest—bull—Oh— one—has—ever known? At—the—same—time (Panting) you know what sex is. Err—Oh—aaaaaaaand (She looked up at the ceiling thoughtfully before she lay on her back on the bed.) How to have sex. Oh, Oh!" She drew him onto her chest. They gazed at each other for only a fraction of a second before she closed her eyes again. He lay over her. His lips moved from her mouth down and round to her breasts, then to her soft and warm flesh. He whispered a few words softly in her ear but she was unable to hear anything; she was in another world. His lips and his finger touches thrilled her beastly. His lips upon hers, she tried to say something but her words had no chance to leave her little mouth. Eventually, the wild thrill she had; the excitement, the joy and the capitulation to definitely irresistible powerful arms crushing her, was immeasurable. Her hands once held his shoulder tips, her nails went deep in his dense flesh and clasped firmly. Their hearts were drumming and their breath was dropping. They were floating high up in heavens chasing the moon and tormenting the stars satisfactorily.

Eleanor felt so tired. She was sweating and panting. Her hands dropped down lifeless to her sides; she went in a snooze. Joseph, breathless, only turned and rolled on his back on the bed beside her. A quarter of an hour later, he came to himself. He looked at her lengthily. "She's a girl of distinction." He said to himself. "She's tall and gorgeous." He liked everything about her, especially her educated language, her breasts, her curved lips, her hair which hung down almost to her waist and her long and thin neck. He wished Gillian had been well educated as Eleanor. Then he would be the happiest husband in the world.

Time slipped fast. It was six-ten pm when Eleanor was dressing. "Oh! Oh! The train's gone." She wailed. "What train? Where're you going?" He asked. "Home, I gonna home. I live in Lateburg." She answered. "What? Lateburg? Don't you live in Hungupville?" Joseph asked amazed or rather disturbed. "No, Sir! I don't!" She answered scornfully, showing no respect. Sharp hatred filled her face. He frowned and said, "Ok, (nodding.) I'll drive you straight to Lateburg. Come on!" He jumped from the bed and dressed hastily.

The road between Hungupville and Lateburg took twenty minutes. They were silent all the time long. When they were turning round a square in Lateburg, there was one of the enemy tanks in the middle of the Martyr Square. Its front was damaged. "Why have they put this tank here?" Joseph asked. "So as not to forget our heroes." Eleanor answered disdainfully. When they arrived at her home, she asked him to drop her. She pointed at a house and said, "Thank you, Sir. That's my house." When she was getting out of the car, Joseph reached in his pocket and pulled out his wallet and said, "Matt complained his revision so early and we wish the train would wait for you up to seven pm. We'll miss you, Eleanor." He handed her three hundred dollars and a 'Bye, bye'. She took the money, smiled ironically, nodded and turned towards her home.

In the morning, when the state departments opened, he got into the Labor Department and then into the Education Department, got an address and a phone number of a new tutor living in Hungupville. Although she hadn't got a degree yet, he preferred her to Eleanor only because she was living in Hungupville.

Gillian came home late at night. She was amazed to find Joseph sound asleep. He had never slept when she was away; outside the house. She undressed, glanced at herself in the mirror and walked to the bed. She tried to awaken him, but he was sound asleep. He was deadbeat that he was snoring. He rolled to the other side but he was unable to wake up. She wanted to tell him about her father, their dinner, and about her parents' garden only! She felt depressed and so she pushed her head further under the blanket trying to sleep. No way! She was tossing and turning in bed for a long time; she kept awake up to early hours in the morning. She had the temptation more than once to awaken him, but she didn't. With all the feminine instincts, she was certain without the faintest doubt that there was something eccentric with Joseph but she didn't dare think there was another woman. The idea was absolutely shocking.

VI

Matthew grew up. In his sixth year at school, he had two tutors. He was really a big boy, intelligent and polite. He hated cheat, deceit and hypocrisy. His friends were jealous of his noble presence, his strong personality, his intelligence and his delicacy. He received individuals and groups of his friends at his home daily. His father felt happy that his son always took the lead when he conversed with his school mates. His mother herself always served them with sandwiches, pies, fruit, peanuts, soft drinks and deserts. The chauffeur had firm instructions to drive each of them back home any time; day or night. Matt rarely paid any of them a visit. He went to their houses only when there was an occasion; a birthday, sickness or a wedding if he was invited although such occasions were rare.

During the vacations that lasted for a week or longer, Mr. and Mrs. Miese, together with their son Matt, drove to the country where they had a house, or they travelled to the capital to their big apartment block. On driving his car, Joseph had never exceeded speed limits; or even the forty-mile-an-hour speed on the highways. He liked the scenic highway to the country. He used to say, "Accidents happen!" Consequently, he had never had any accident whatever small it was. Whenever he sensed danger, he parked his car at a rest stop, had a break and relaxed. They admired the scenery. As the trees offered welcome shade from the sun, Joseph lay down on a mattress they had for picnics and leaned upon his elbow. Meanwhile, they didn't waste time. They had their video camera in addition to their mobile-phone cams to take photographs of everything they liked; anything odd and any living thing moved they caught sight of. Gillian and Joseph always liked Matt asking his father, "Gimme a piggy-back, Daddy!" Joseph liked to be a horse and Matt the rider. When he hopped, the three of them laughed long.

Matthew had never been allowed to go far away from his parents. A hundred feet were so far and a long distance. Nor was he allowed to go swimming alone. Even with a company, his father or any trusted person had to circle the place swimming to check any possible danger. Matthew was always patient, "Five-minute late is all the same." He said. When Joseph heard him, he always said, "There's a big similarity between Matt and his Grandpa. Not only Matt looks after him, but both are intelligent, patient, educated and humanitarian!" "Why don't you tell me much about my grandpa, Dad? Wasn't he a paragon of his country?" Matt asked. Joe gave a faint smile that gestured sorrow and despair. "Your Grandpa was well educated and a real humanitarian. He was called out twice by the army but he had never aimed at any living thing when he had his arm in his hand. He wasn't a coward, but he knew well that wars were fought at random. War and democracy don't match, he used to say."

Matt was shooting up fast. His acquired traits were developing quickly. When he was in his final year in Hungupville High School, he was seventeen. His success was safe. Success alone wouldn't satisfy him nor would it satisfy his parents. He should get the highest points; the maximum. It was unacceptable for all of them that Matt would be the second in his school, or even in the whole Hungupville schools; state or private. His tutors, his teachers, his friends and his classmates all were certain that Matt would get the highest points. Joseph was quite certain that Matt had one of the great minds of the age; a real scientist's or a VIP's.

VII

All of Matt's classmates; males or females, were close friends to him except one; only one student. She was Pamela Sompler. Pamela (Pam) was seventeen, too. She descended from an ordinary family. Her mother was an employee in a house-cleaning company and her father, Bruce Sompler, was an officer in Hungupville Police-Unit. Bruce received a rescue phone-call from an old lady who was living alone in a shed at the edge of the forest and whom he had acquainted with in the hospital when his wife was giving birth to Pamela. "Help me! Help me, Mr. Sompler! There's a terrible reptile in my shed." The old lady pleaded with him. Before Bruce was able to ask about more information or say anything, she hung up the phone. Mr. Sompler held his gun and with a jerk from his head, the jeep driver followed him. They drove fast to the old lady's place. Bruce glimpsed a child who looked like his own daughter; Pam. He ordered the driver to stop and to reverse the jeep a few feet; to the crossing. It was Pam walking aimlessly far from home. She was nine years old. Her father put her beside him in the jeep and drove to the old lady's shed.

When the driver stopped the car opposite to the shed, and the engine was off, Mr. Sompler got out and walked towards the door which was suddenly opened and three mobsters got out of it holding their machine guns and stood in a row opposite to him and to his driver. Pamela was still in the jeep. "Hay, Cop! Your wife's beautiful. I like her. Do you think she'll marry me soon after your funeral?" One of them said aloud and the three men roared with laughter. What that gangster said was intolerable for Bruce Sompler. He held his gun and, instantly, the three guns went off. Showers of shots were fired out. Mr. Sompler wasn't killed at once but he fell down. The three men walked to him and the same man said, "Don't worry! There'll be two bouquets of flowers on your grave on the wedding day!" And he fired another shower of shots.

Pamela got out of the jeep crying and wailing. She hurried to her father and hugged him. "Take me home, Dad! Take me home!" She implored. One of the killers kicked her away and said, "You'll have a new father so soon, kid." The three men got into the jeep and drove to the woods leaving Pam alone with the two dead bodies. She returned to her father and bent on his head crying and wailing.

The old lady got out of her shed leaning on her walking stick. Her face, as well as her legs, was bleeding heavily. She walked straight to the child, hugged her and said, "Oh dear. Those rogues threatened to kill my son, my grandchildren and burn me and my shed if I didn't make that phone call."

Some Hungupvillian heard the shooting. Two police-patrol jeeps and an ambulance came to the crime field. The old lady repeated the same story which she had narrated to Pam and described her attackers to the police. The ambulance took the old lady and the child to the hospital. Another ambulance was called to carry the two corpses. The old lady was rescued as her cuts were not so serious but Pam was unable to speak. Psychiatrists were consulted and she needed three weeks to recover.

Whenever she was at home and one of her mother's male acquaintances came, she thought they were taking her mother away from her and she hugged her and cried. "Don't go with'em, Mom. Please Mom, don't go. They'll kill you." Pamela implored her mom. It was a complexity that she suffered for years. Anyway, the police could draw pictures of the killers upon Pamela's and the old lady's counts but they were unable to stop any of them.

Mrs. Sompler, who was thirty years old when her husband was killed, declined to get married. She sacrificed the pleasures of life to take care of her daughter; Pamela. She rejected generous offers from elite members so as not to be detached from her child.

As she was unable to afford a private car and a chauffeur when Pam was a big girl in the high school, Pam moved to and fro between her house and her school by bus. Her dignity and her pride forbade her to implore any of the wealthy students to give her a lift or to accept their offers, which were not out of hypocrisy, regardless of the dusty and hot weather in summer or in the stormy cold winter.

Although Pam had never been dressed in fashion, her outfitting was chosen properly. It was neat, gratifying and respectable. Overall, she looked attractive. She was living a simple life and she had never felt jealous of the wealthy males or females of her classmates. She was a determined and an aspired girl who had the absolute will to pass her exams with an excellent ranking. Her way to college was to get a scholarship. Otherwise, her mom was unable to afford for college whatever the specialization was. Pam was hardworking and intelligent as well as Matthew Miese, but she had never got a higher point than his.

Pamela Sompler was 'Miss Hungupville High School' without any competitor. She always sailed across the classroom when she was getting in or out, but she had never been heard or seen laughing although she always smiled. Although her smile was mostly meaningful, it was the sweetest smile one had ever seen. She had never shouted or spoken aloud. When she raised her hand to ask or answer a question, silence reigned in the classroom. One could hear a pin dropping on the floor. Her elegancy, intelligence and self-respect were unique and incomparable in Hungupville. All her female classmates were jealous of her beauty, gravity, intelligence and of her strong personality. She was really a dear; an angel of pure beauty that she knew well she had been the most sought girl in the town. She hardly had a close friend although all her classmates; males and females, wished her friendship. Matthew as well as all his male classmates longed to win her heart or at least to exchange a word with her. Whenever he tried, he got a smile, only a smile, without a single word. "Riches don't always satisfy!" He murmured.

Mathew Miese went to the principal's office in his school upon the latter's request. The principal was out of his office and so the secretary told Matt to wait for him in the sitting room as he was coming back so soon. After five minutes, Pamela Sompler came to the secretary asking her about the principal. She, too, had to sit in the same room and to wait for him. Matt and Pam were surprised. It was the first time they were face to face alone. They side looked at each other shyly without saying any word. Since the secretary couldn't hear any word coming out from the sitting room, she went to the kitchen and brought two glasses of tea on a tray; one was for Pam and the other for Matt. She forgot herself and so she returned to the kitchen to bring a third glass. Meantime, Pam lifted her head and looked towards Matt to say something but she changed her mind when the secretary came in. To start a conversation, the secretary said that the principal was on his way to school. Although both of them wished the other had said any word, none of them was dare enough to say anything.

In a minute, the principal arrived and got into his office. He received them smiling. Then he pointed at two adjoining seats and gestured to them to be seated. His eyes moved from one to the other when he asked them which more worthy was to chase: learning and high study or job-seeking and money-making. His question was striking. None of them had the answer ready in his head. Matthew looked at Pamela who was looking at him. Both sought help from the other mutually and mutely. Their eyes said; not their tongues or their lips. Then Matt initiated, "I suppose we're meant to intuit the answer although we're still young and we haven't experienced life yet. Anyway, I feel that money, little or much shouldn't keep one from getting what one's aiming at; learning and science." Both of Pam and the principal thought that it seemed he hadn't given money much consideration. Matt wished that his words had been enough to answer the principal's question. He felt he had to say something because he was a male, and he did. A male should be more courageous than a female. It would be shameful to implore Pam to say anything. Then he looked at Pam who was listening amazed. She had a faint smile on her face. As well as Matt, she gave a sigh of relief. She seemed to be attracted to Matt, not on the account of his rich family, but because his words were always simple and natural. The principal told them he was going to meet with the seniors for the last time next week. He wished they would have prepared general questions concerning all of them and those questions should be submitted to his office in two days. Matt stood up, thanked the principal and walked to the door. Pam followed him. He opened the door and stood aside. She smiled, raised her brows, opened her eyes wide, nodded and crossed the door out. Then she screwed her head round, smiled at him and nodded again when she was three steps away. He didn't believe his eyes that he stood still holding the door handle. He stretched his head out through the door giving her a farewell look but she didn't see him. When the principal coughed a little, Matt came to himself again. He turned his head towards the principal, nodded and got out. He crossed the school yard to the gate and got out. In the car parking, he looked for the chauffeur and for their car, but he couldn't see either of them. He was dialing the chauffeur's cellular number when he felt someone patting him on the shoulder. Matt looked over his shoulder to find the principal himself standing close to him. He asked Matt whether he was fine. Matt couldn't say anything. He only nodded thoughtless. The principal thought a little. He was sure that Matt was scatter-brained. He smiled and ordered him firmly, "Go back to your Chemistry Class!" "Chemistry Class?" Matt repeated thoughtlessly. Suddenly, he remembered. The school hadn't finished yet and the chauffeur hadn't been waiting for him. He smacked his forehead, apologized and hurried back to his Chemistry Class.

Pam was there. She was worried that there might be some more conversation between the principal and Matt behind her back. Matt had never been late to classes and so she felt jealous and curios; she looked anxious.

When Matt got into the Chemistry Classroom, he sat on a chair next to her, close to the door. She didn't have the courage to ask him, or her pride stood between her and her curiosity. Matt gave her a stream of constant side looks; he didn't take his eyes off her; nor did she. They looked at each other mutually. Seeing her absent-minded, he knew what she was thinking of, but she didn't take notice of his looks. He smiled cunningly and nodded. As well as Pam, he wasn't listening to the teacher; he was busy thinking of her.

VIII

G illian had never been ill-dressed. Her preferable color was white or light pink for the outfitting and any dark color for the close-fitting. Her favorite perfume was lavender. She always dressed in the latest fashion that she thought of appearance more than she thought of her son, her husband or her house. When someone commented that would cost a lot of money and it would be boring to dress and undress times a day, she said, "Nothing satisfies Joe. He always complains that I look shabby whenever he sees me in the same clothing twice a day. It pleases him to look beautiful and to be always dressed in the latest fashion. Any loyal wife should always think how to please her husband." Although she was right, she shifted the blame to other shoulders. She was a woman who was showing off.

Every morning, when Joseph went to his factory and Matthew left for school, Gillian walked in the garden holding her basket in her hand and pruned the flower bushes, watered them or picked enough flowers to fill a vase. She also filled the basket with chosen ripe fruits. She used to tell her mother when she rang her and the women who called her that the tulips were blossoming and they were wonderful. The trees, too, were budding, and then flowering and finally the fruits were getting ripe in her garden. She rejected hiring a gardener as gardening was one of her recreations and she did that outdoor activity without her gloves, coveralls or even pants on. When she got back into the bathroom around noon, her hands were covered with scratches and her white garments had been stained with black, green and brown stains. She always said that Joe liked her shaped legs. He used to say, "Your well-shaped legs match with your Miss-World waist!" Therefore she didn't need to hide them.

In winter when it was freezing, she shoveled the snow and the fallen leaves from the garden walks. She also shoveled a walk to the front entrance of their villa by herself with only a pink T-shirt and a white skirt which had never reached her knee down, without pants or a raincoat on. When she finished and got into the house, she trembled. Her lips were bluish red. She shivered, sneezed and coughed. When her son Matt told her that she had better wear heavier clothes, she was shocked and gazed at him angrily saying, "Too ugly or too old am I?" Then she added only to soften her tone, "Anyway, it took a few minutes only!"

In his late adolescence and early twenties before Gillian attracted him, Joseph was straight and he spent his life collecting money. After marriage, he was a straight husband, too. He believed that the fool only had time to love. Therefore, he was a hardworking and successful businessman. Nevertheless, neither had he considered himself, nor he was considered by anyone else that he had been one of the businessmen. When businessmen, industrialists, merchants, bankers, or commission dealers met as equals, he didn't equate any of them, out of money making, in education and in the relentless pursuit of sex, adventure and power.

On the contrary of them, he completely missed all that worthless stuff; as he always said. He spent most of his time at work in his store then in his factory with his employees. However, if he had to go out to enjoy himself, he would lose a lot, he thought. Anyway, he always felt there was something missing in his life but he had never thought it was adventure or love out of the family bedroom. He was unable to know that human nature ordained all people had the same needs including vacations, friendship and enjoyment of something or another. A life which was only to get money, and more money, far from other people, could never bring pleasure, happiness or security. Those things together with the admiration of others couldn't be bought by money. Life should be colorful. He had no friends; neither did he try to attract any woman before Gillian. Eleanor was the second although she wasn't his love or his girlfriend as he wasn't her man. She was only an outlet for an exceeding energy.

IX

Joseph was always alone and he felt bored in his office in the factory. Therefore he ordered that his computer should be connected to the Internet a few days ago. He could waste much time on the home page reading various news and ads. Someday, he got this advertisement *'Do you want a university degree? You can get your BA, MA or PHD online in less than two years!' You can click* (www.some initials and consequent connected words which looked as if they were a meaningless long one.) He clicked that site which opened at once. At the bottom of the page, there was a form to be filled in. They required name, sex, age, last college or school level, phone number, email ID and a physical address. There was also a list of specializations from which one had to choose a subject. He was amazed. Could he get a university degree so easily and so quickly? He didn't trust his eyes. He read again but it was unbelievable. By getting a degree, Mr. Miese thought, he'd be on equal terms with his colleagues; the industrialists in the area. He decided to go to the Department of Education in Hungupville Municipality. It was the first time he found out that one could study online and get a degree. It was open for literate people; regardless of their previous grade at school or college. He left his office earlier than usual and drove straight to the

Department of Education. On the road, he was very happy. He was dreaming that he fancied himself Professor J. Miese. He compared between Gillian with the University-Of-Life Degree and Eleanor with her BA Degree. He burst with laughter and murmured, "If Gill were as well educated as Eleanor, I'd find the utmost happiness with her." The fact was that Gillian was more beautiful than Eleanor and she was loyal to her husband; she adored him.

In the Education Department, he asked the man in charge whether one could study via Internet, read books, take examinations and get a degree. The answer was that one could. Joseph was suspicious and cautious. On his way home, he thought why he didn't go to the university and ask them. He looked at his watch. It was still early. He drove fast to the university and asked them the same question. The answer was positive. They thought of something but he was talking about another different thing. He got their phone number and went straight to his house and then to his PC in the study. He turned it on and went to the same site again where he read he would take his first exam in a few months. Another few months, he had to take the finals. His BA Degree was guaranteed. So, he would study day and night. He was longing for that degree. He rang Hungupville University and asked them how long one needed to get the first university degree. The answer was three years or over. He added, "All Universities and all faculties?" "No, not all universities. That depe . . ." He interrupted the speaker and said, "Thank you. Bye, bye." and hung up. He asked about the online study, but the answer was about the state universities.

He was sure that he was able to get his BA Degree online in time. Therefore, he filled in the form with only one item missing; an email ID! He chose to specialize in 'English Language'. He typed his credit-card details to pay for the whole course of study. Then they redirected him to another site where he could read books and do samples of the examination questions. On that site, he found poetry, drama, prose, criticism, literary works of English and foreign writers, schools of literature, History of the English Language . . . . And he was unable to read correctly the titles of the classic Greek and Roman literary works which were translated into English, their writers' names or the names of their characters which were either old Greek or Latin. The first thing he chose to read was Literary Criticism but he couldn't understand a single sentence. "Why are all these puzzles?" He murmured. He used to criticize others and he heard others criticizing everyone and everything but that English criticism on that site was different.

After supper, he went back to his PC. He turned it on and went to the same site. As there was a lot of drama on TV, he tried drama hoping he could get something, but he really got nothing. What would he do with those puzzles? There wouldn't be a degree without studying hard; he thought. Who would teach him? Who would explain those Sino-Sanskrit texts? He sat opposite to his computer and supported his head on his hand on the PC table. He looked depressed and preoccupied. What he wanted was to scrap through the final exams only.

Gillian was lying awake in her bedroom, listening to the clock announcing one after midnight. She wondered what Joe was doing in the study. Busy minded, she rose up with only her long, light and hung nightgown on. It was purple, low-backed and its collar went down below her breast parting. She paused opposite to the mirror, smoothened down her hair, darkened her lips, sprayed a little scent on some spots of her soft body and walked barefooted to the study. On her way in the corridor, she saw the light on in Matthew's room; he was still studying and so she gave a sigh of relief. Then she went on to the study. Joseph was sitting in his seat opposite to his computer doing nothing. She leaned on his broad shoulders, extended her hands over them, wiped his chest and said softly, "What's the matter, Joe? You've been sitting here for long hours."

Joseph came to himself. He held her hands and drew her half a turn round his seat. She sat in his lap with her right arm around his neck. Joseph told her the whole story when his two arms wrapped her waist. "It is incredible. Joseph would get a degree!" She said to herself amazed. "Could you repeat what you have just said, please?" She asked. He looked at her with a sardonic laugh which became bigger and louder that he roared with laughter and said, "You'll be the only uneducated one in our family! Matt will take his finals in a few months then he'll go to the university. Another few months, I'll get my BA. And you? Is the University of Life enough for you?" He paused a little and looked in her eyes. Then he added, "Don't worry! I'll be all the same. You'll stay my love; my only love." His lips passed on her neck and he bit her earlobe softly and whispered, "Could you make me a glass of tea, please?" She rose up stunned. On her way to the kitchen, she was muttering away to herself and shaking her head, "Joe'll get a degree in less than two years! How is that?" She stopped for a moment. "Unbelievable! He left school when he was twelve. I did when I was fourteen. I'd do better in the university than what he'd do." She continued while making tea. When she returned to the study, there were two glasses of tea on the tray. Joseph smiled mockingly and said, "Let me guess what you thought! You'd do better . . ." She interrupted defiantly but smiled childishly, "Yes, I did. Don't you think I'd do better than what you may do at college? I went to school two years more than you did! I dream of spending a couple of hours in a health farm. I dream of being a social activist. I dream of dancing in a night club. I dream of being a member in the National Woman League (NWL). I dream of participating in an antiwar demonstration. Only educated women take share in those activities although I'm richer, more beautiful and more elegant than them. If your father were alive, you'd be a politician, a Representative in the House, a senior officer or a university or college professor. Didn't you like to be one of them?" Gillian said regretfully and tears filled her eyes. Joe opened his mouth and eyes wide. Not a word could get out of his mouth. Then he nodded and sighed. For a moment, silence prevailed in the study. Then he looked as if he remembered something. "You're right, Gill. Absolutely right! My father was a graduate and he wanted me to be well-educated, but the reserve, the auxiliaries, the pacts and wars always stopped in our face depriving us from achieving our aspirations. I wish he were alive until I was granted my high school diploma." Joseph said sorrowfully. "What specialization are you going to study?" Gillian asked. He answered without hesitation, "English. I can read, write and speak English and so it will be easy to study a subject I know!" She commented, "So can I. I've got long free time daily. Let's study together." "Really?" He inquired. "Do you mean it?" He added amazed. "Yes, I do. I mean it.

Joe, stop mocking at me!" Instantly, he went to the same site again and Gillian filled in the form. Then she tried to read something, but she found that was very difficult to understand. "What's this, Joe? Is this the English Language we speak?" She was surprised. "What seems to be easy to some people (patting on his chest), seems to be difficult to others." Joseph said boasting and giving her a side look. She knew she was aimed at by the hint. She didn't react at once but she smirked and said to herself, "We'll see who'll do better!" Both rose up. Gillian bent down to turn the computer off. When she stood erect, he carried her on his arms and headed to the bedroom.

Joseph was sound asleep in ten minutes. Gillian couldn't. She thought deep of the university, of the degree and of Joseph. She wished she had chosen a different subject. "I'd have chosen History. I know a lot about History. The news is a good teacher." She thought. "Joe!" She called and looked in his face. He was sound asleep, and so she felt frustrated.

Gillian was more cautious and more jealous than her husband. In the morning, when they were sitting at the breakfast table, she said, "Joe, it occurred to me that English was really a wrong choice. Can I change to History?" Matthew, as well as his father, was surprised. He smiled thoughtfully. Then he asked, "Mom, you're not going to study at a college, are you?" She waited for Joseph to say something but he kept silent. So, she nodded. Then his father said questioningly, "Why not?" "And you, too, Dad?" Matt asked amazed. "Yes, I am. We both will study and get a degree online." Joe answered. "But, Dad, you didn't go to the high school. And that degree online . . ." His father interrupted, "I need it badly. I'm not going to be a teacher.

So is Gill. It's only a prestige." "But Dad . . ." "You haven't dressed yet! You'll be tardy for school." Gill interrupted. The three of them rose up.

On his way to school, Matthew thought long of his parents. They were right. They'll take advantage of their free time and get some education. They were rich enough to have a country house and a big building in the capital in addition to their Miese Butter, Cheese & Cream Factory. Their future was secure. They missed a little bit of education only. That was on one hand. On the other, they would be the disdain of the town. Most of the inhabitants of Hungupville liked a bit of scandal and the Mieses were well known to every one of them. Then he shrugged carelessly and dismissed the whole idea from his vision. It was a hard headache.

X

Joseph was busy in his office looking for a file in the cabinet behind his chair. A woman, in her early thirties, quite tall, well built with black eyes, dark face, short auburn hair and a yellow knee coat entered the office without knocking at the open door. She stood contemplating Joe amazed. "What a wrestler!" She murmured raising her eyebrows and licking her lips. She put her handbag on the coffee table and advanced to his desk silently gazing at him with open mouth and eyes. Joseph turned suddenly. Unknowing there was somebody in his room; he was surprised to see her.

"Good morning. Can I help you?" He addressed her. She smiled sweetly and coquettishly. Her smile and her face expressions were so sexy. She stepped forward extending her hand out and said, "Joseph Miese, right?" He nodded. "Jocelyn Dang." She introduced herself, still smiling. "Dang?" He inquired, pointing with his finger meaning Robert Dang, a worker in his factory. She nodded. He shook hands with her, "Nice to meet you, Jocelyn?" He pointed with his hand to a seat on his right saying, "Be seated, please."

She undid the coat buttons and sat crossing her legs when a light purple micro mini skirt showed up covering nothing of her thighs. As she crossed her arms on her chest,

Joseph was unable to see her upper half which the coat had covered completely. She noticed Joseph eyeballing her and a faint smile appeared on her face. She said to herself, "He must be dissatisfied sexually."

Robert Dang was an uncommitted voter. As parties appealed to such uncommitted people, and to get their votes in the elections, they asked Mr. Dang whom he would vote for, but he hadn't decided then. When they asked him what his job was, he said he was a job seeker. And so they promised him of a job if he voted for them. To keep their promises, political parties sent those people to firms owned by their fan clubs. The party would pay their wages for the first ninety days only. Then it was optional to the employer to dismiss or to keep them; on their own expense. Robert Dang was lucky to keep his job as Mr. Miese needed laborers badly then. Robert Dang had been told that his partner had been waiting for him in the president's office. He puffed, left what he was doing, had his coat on and walked quickly to the same office.

He was a fat man, bald and quite short. He looked uncool in his shabby garments. Although he looked very tired, his eyes shone incomprehensively. At least, he was twenty years senior to Jocelyn. He took his hat off and started, "Excuse me, Sir! Jocelyn's come to ask about my salary. She doesn't believe what I get is hardly enough to afford her own expenses. She always complains. Six months ago, when I brought her my first salary in full, she kissed me. (Laughing and pointing at his cheek, not at his lips.) An hour later, she cried and said that I didn't think she was beautiful. She left home and spent the night away." She interrupted boldly and frankly, turning her black eyes upon him, "Money's the most important thing in the world; more important than many people!" Robert Dang dropped his head and continued, "Yesterday evening, she asked me showers of questions about you and about your business. I told her you were kind, athlete, handsome, sociable and a well-educated youth and very rich. (Joseph sat up on his chair and flattened his chest.) Then she asked for ten dollars although she knew well I hadn't got a single buck. She quarreled with me and left home. Quarreling and leaving home is an item on her half-weekly agenda. In the morning, I found her lying on the sofa recliner. She had been drunk."

"Ok, Mr. Dang. Go back to work! I'll send for you later. Let me talk to Jocelyn." Joseph said. Robert left the room and got back to his work. Jocelyn, who was almost silent all the time when Robert was talking, said, "You shouldn't take anything he said at face value." Then she stood up turning her back to Joe and started to take off her coat. Joseph stood up and took it off her shoulders but he stuck to his place amazed when he saw her in a lace tulle flying babydoll. She pushed him to hang the coat behind the door. Although she was without a bra, her breasts didn't know where the south was. Her scent and deodorant smelled thrillingly. She turned and one hand was closing and locking the door and the other was checking Joe's arm softly. Then she whispered, "Athlete!" When one of his arms wrapped her waist, she unbuttoned her skirt which fell on the carpet and a thrilling little transparent V-thong showed up; although every piece of her clothing was thrilling. His other hand was patting and brushing her buttocks and their lips stuck to each other's. He fell right into her trap.

Jocelyn and Joseph looked as if they were in love and they had been dating each other since a long time. He carried her on his arms as if she were a little child and whispered in her ear, "Venus!" Hearing that word, she wrapped his neck with her arms. Soon, she was lying on the sofa recliner and Joe was lying on her with their mouths stuck to each other's and their hands brushing, probing, circling, wiping and holding something or another of the other. The long 'Ohs and Ahs' were repeated many times and their resounds waved in the room. Eventually, they were breathless, speechless and they lay deadbeat for long, long minutes.

Joe dropped down and lay on the carpet but she was still lying subconscious on the sofa when she gasped, "That gay's murdering me." She unburdened herself to him. It was an indication aimed at Robert Dang, her partner. "Is he?" Joe asked amazed. She nodded and said, "Another victim of prisons." She was quite tired unable to add any more word. Joseph was still amazed. He thought a little before he asked, "What did he do?" After a long pause, she said, "He was in love with an Eastern woman and travelled to the East to meet her but the IGA stopped him there. His accusation was espionage. He spent years in their prisons. You know him well now. Is he fit to be one of the intelligence service men?"

Half an hour later, she put her underwear in her handbag. Then she dressed her skirt and her coat, brushed her hair, lit a cigarette and curled her legs under her. Joe opened the door and ordered two cups of coffee and then he returned to his chair behind his desk. When the tray was on the coffee table, he left his chair and sat in a seat opposite to Jocelyn who was still sitting on the sofa. He was smiling with satisfaction when his eyes were in hers. He took his cup and had a sip. "In all of the past years of work and money making, I didn't have any cup of coffee more delicious than this. It's really yummy! I'm delighted to have it with you Jocelyn before Robert returns. How tasty it is!" Jocelyn smiled cunningly and said softly, "Joe! Is it the coffee or is it something else?" She aimed at her lips. She dropped her eyes shyly but her fingers went to her coat's buttons and undid them. Joseph smirked, opened his eyes wide and raised his eyebrows. Then he extended his two hands to her knees, then a little higher and higher to her inner thighs and to her soft flesh. "Oh, Joe! Your fingers are thrilling!" She said and opened her eyes to see the door still open. "The door! The door, Joe! It's open!" She said aloud and lay on the sofa. Joe hurried to the door, slammed and locked it. When he returned, her coat was thrown down on the carpet. Joe threw his heavy but thrilling body on her. Then his arms wrapped her waist and his face went down to her lips and it moved lower and lower. His fingers went high up again and disappeared in her thick and short hair. Then the only thing she could do was to gasp, "Oh, Joe! What a bull you are!" A few minutes later; when she had the strength to speak, she asked, "Tell me please, how many women did you seduce?" She was smiling maliciously. He thought he was insulted and degraded; he wasn't a loyal husband. So, he stretched his hand into his wallet in his pocket and handed her a twenty-dollar bill. She snatched it and straight into her wallet in her handbag.

She was surprised to find her close fittings still in her handbag, and so she had to put them on. Joe was observing her before he answered back, "Is it the first bill today?" She, having her tail between her legs, didn't answer. She only hung her head in shame. "Why don't you help Robert?" He added and gazed at her. She gazed at him unpleasantly. Then she gave him a mocking half-smile and answered back, "I'm a woman! Why don't you help him?" She recognized well that Joseph aimed at Robert's financial situation but as his educational and his cultural powers were not so polished, he was unable to understand her goal behind her question; he completely missed the point of her aim.

"And didn't you exchange presents last Christmas?" Joseph asked. "Christmas, as a special day, had never been special to me. Oh, how painful to be poor! People with spouses, children, parents, siblings and friends give and get so lovely things." She said dolefully and looked in Joe's face with eyes blurred with tears. Joseph said bitterly, "You reminded me with my mother. When I was ten and my father was away in Asia, I cried on that Christmas to get a present; a toy gun, but she said we shouldn't celebrate while Dad was suffering away in his camp somewhere in Asia. Oh, it was a hard time!"

On her way out, she looked over her shoulder and said, "Adonis!" "What time are you coming tomorrow?" He asked. "Same time!" She said laughing. Just at the door of the office when she was getting out, Joseph said, "There wasn't enough seasoning in the broth, although delicious!" And he winked at her. She thought a second, smiled, nodded, winked at him and waved her hand, 'Bye, bye.'

Joseph sent for Mr. Dang again. Robert Dang knocked at the door, entered Mr. Miese's office and started, "Yes, Sir!" "Sit down, Robert." Joseph said gesturing to him to sit in one of the seats but Robert walked and sat on the same sofa recliner on which his woman was lying minutes ago and said, "Thank you, Sir!" "Why on that sofa, not in the seat?" Joseph asked. "I know that Jocelyn was lying on this sofa. She loves lying on sofas. I like to replace her because I love her! We often replaced each other in the North Mountain Base (NMB)! Did she lie here, Sir, on this sofa?" Joseph was unable to guess what Robert aimed at exactly! Any way, he said, "Look Robert! You're here as an employee. You receive your salary on time. We can hire a youth for your salary. Youths can carry heavier burdens twice or three times of what you can. I don't know how you have the face to complain of your little salary when you do so little work. Unfortunately, there's no place for sentiment in business. (Thoughtful.) Well, if Jocelyn can do something on the computer, we'll find her a job in the secretarial section. You can help each other. One of the women in the secretarial section is leaving next week. Jocelyn may replace her." Joseph said seriously. "I may be an old man, Sir, but I'm not senile yet. I confess I've never surprised her with a present. That's behind my capacity. I can't afford all that she wants. Although she isn't very reliable, I like her all the same. Thanks for the offer, Sir. I'll talk to Jocelyn this evening."

When Joseph went home in the afternoon, and he was sitting at the dinner table, he ate a lot; more than usual, but he was very tired and he felt sleepy. He was yawning and tears fell down from his eyes. At first, Gillian was very happy to see him with a sharp appetite. She said to him teasingly, "You eat with a sharp appetite! A soldier in vacation!" But her blood boiled when his eyes sank down and his face darkened, "I always feel hungry when I taste the food you cook!" He said, rose up and walked straight to the bedroom. In twenty years, it was the first time Joe preceded her to the bedroom. After ten minutes, she followed him. He was sound asleep. She stood stunned with a darkened face. "Was he tired of a hard work or was there another woman?" She wondered. "It should be a woman." She murmured. It's feminine intuition.

On the second day, Joseph was in his office sitting at his computer trying to change Gillian's specialization from English to History when he heard someone knocking at the open door. When he raised his head up, Jocelyn Dang had come in and she was walking to his desk. She was in a navy unstrapped mini dress. Joseph started, "Good morning, Jocelyn. They're waiting for you in the secretarial section. Could you fill in a job-application form there, please?" She nodded and turned back heading to the secretarial section. Then he rang the executive secretary to keep Jocelyn with them after she would have filled in the form. He added in a low voice, "The application should be on my desk as soon as it was completed."

Jocelyn went to the secretarial section and introduced herself as Jocelyn Cherries. The executive secretary received her with a smile and said, "Nice to meet you, Jocelyn. I'm Christina. Have a seat, please." Christina was giving her a side look when she stretched her hand to take an application form from a file cabinet next to her desk. Jocelyn didn't look a woman seeking a job. She looked rich of a noble family. She was dressing in fashion and she had come from a beauty salon. Christina handed her the form and a pen. Jocelyn completed it in a minute and rose up when the phone rang. Christina gave her a sign to sit down when she answered the phone. It was Mr. Miese asking about Jocelyn's application which she didn't have time to read yet. She hasted to her president's office holding the application in her hand and giving a gesture to her colleague to order a drink for Jocelyn. Joseph took it and asked her opinion with Jocelyn. "Sir, I don't think she's come seeking a job. She must have paid a month salary for the beauty salon."

Joseph didn't hear all that Christina had said. He was reading the application. Jocelyn was a graduate! She had been a school teacher in Hungupville High School for five years before she resigned three years ago. He nodded and murmured, "Great!" and told Christina to send Jocelyn back to his office.

Christina left the room and went back to her office. When Jocelyn came in, she turned to lock the door but Joseph stopped her. "Please Jocelyn, let's have a word first." Jocelyn obeyed. She stepped to his desk and sat on it leaning to kiss him. He gave no resistance and responded well. "Be seated, please." Joseph said pointing with his hand at a seat close to his desk. She got down the desk and sat in the same seat that Joseph pointed at. Her legs long almost showed up. While he was shutting his PC off, he asked, "Jocelyn, are you really a graduate?" His eyes were still on the application.

Jocelyn felt unrest as he hadn't given her much consideration yet. He was reading what she had written. "Yes, I'm, Sir!" She smiled faintly but horror filled her eyes. Then she added, "I was single when I was a teacher in the high school. I was fired out because of that agreeable guy whom you, Hungupvillians, appointed my boss. He was honest and loyal to his wife. I see no bang of conscience at loving another woman's husband. Any man can admire a woman's tenderness, beauty and passion and can be loyal and true to his wife. But it wasn't a question of honesty or loyalty. It was a question of inability. He reported me to the principal and I was fired." She said laughing and winked at him. Then she commented, "I don't find it humiliating, defecting or shameful to flirt with and make love to the married men and they stay faithful and loyal to their wives, do you, Joe?"

Her manner and her behavior had their own measurements; she was quite unconcerned with the questions of morality. None was faithful as far as that served her goals. Then she went on saying, "Is it shameful to love and make love with the military body in the NMB? They Miss their wives and their wives miss them. After the demonstrations against the NMB, we lost a lot. Neither the army personnel were allowed to leave the base nor we were allowed going there and the soldiers had to spend their vacations abroad. I was homeless, jobless and penniless for more than a year when I met Robert in a bar. I caught him gazing at my legs. I had no choice then as I was at the very end of my tethers. I undid the two buttons of my skirt, although it was one foot over knee, and crossed my legs. He drew nearer to me and asked whether I needed company. I smiled and nodded. After brushing my knees, and a little of my inner thighs softly, he made me an offer to be partners. After a short talk, I accepted although I was sure that not a woman could look at him twice but I was between the devil and the deep blue sea. I fell behind with the rent and I was evicted. I didn't have any interest in his person; I was interested in some serious relation with anyone to get out of my trouble. I had him to get shelter and personal expenses, you know (winking). Unfortunately, I found myself living worse conditions than the life I had to quit. We live under adobe and hay ceiling. He had me as an ornament to complete his manhood although it was completely missing. He was gazing at me in the bar stimulated by curiosity, not by sex hunger. That was two years ago." She was crying and smiling. Joseph was listening attentively. Then she said, "How much does man take from life? Nothing!" She paused a little before she added, "Or a little bit." She blew her nose and concluded, "Sometimes, I ask myself what sort of a man I would be if I weren't a woman! I'd certainly be wretched, too." She smiled ironically and looked in Joseph's eyes. Then she sighed regretfully and wiped her eyes.

Joseph engaged himself in Jocelyn's application for a few minutes during which she could remember her entire life!

At age sixteen, Jocelyn looked sweet and charming. In reality, she was hopeless and cheeky. She had never had a boyfriend or a girlfriend. Nevertheless, she never felt she needed those people. Her father was proud of his poverty as the Mieses were proud of their wealth. He was fired more than once from his work because he was a wino. Even when he risked his life and worked in the NMB as a waiter in their canteen, he couldn't stop drinking although he was warned many times not to drink when he was on duty; consequently he was fired. Only a few months before he died, he had only one glass of wine after supper and that was upon the doctors' warning. He left her nothing behind him when he died. She lived with her mother in a poky little room in Hungupville. Her mother died a little more than a year after her father. She was paralyzed living on the state welfare. By her death, Jocelyn's world fell apart. She was a student at Hungupville University then, and so she lost that little money her mother supplied her and the place where she lived. She suffered poverty in her childhood and in her adolescence and then in her youth. She had to depend upon herself to afford her study and her own expenses. Although she tried hard and implored for any job in Hungupville, she couldn't get more than a waitressing or a servicing one in a Hungupvillian café house. Undergraduate and unskilled Hungupvillian women weren't lucky to find jobs and they were threatened to risk their lives if they got any job in the NMB.

Jocelyn was an easy hunt for those who claimed wealth. She left her work and followed them; one after another. When she found out their realities, she tried to go back to the same café house, then to other café houses and to restaurants but that was impossible as she was defamed. She thought of Lateburg; the nearest town to Hungupville, but she couldn't work there as it was far from the university and it was hard to find a vacancy there. Finally, she thought it would be more profitable if she depended upon her beauty and upon her youth. And so she spent the nights between the arms of different men and slept in the daytime. Therefore, she couldn't attend the minimum lectures to complete her study and get her first university degree. Consequently, she was expelled from the university.

When her colleagues were taking their finals, a retired ex-employee in the university offered to provide her a BA Degree for spending three months with him as his girlfriend. She was unable to decline. The oral contract between them came fully to its end, and so he gave her the promised degree and then she was appointed a teacher in Hungupville High School.

Five years later, one of her previous colleagues was appointed a supervisor in that school. He had known she had been expelled from college and he remembered her story in detail. When she was called into his office to answer some questions about her resume', she tried to seduce him. As everyone has their price, she offered to receive him for a month as a guest and a lover, but he was married and he declined. Then she offered to give him half of her salary for a year, but he declined, too. And then he offered her to resign and he would keep his mouth shut. As she had no choice, she accepted; she resigned and left the school. By her resignation, she turned back to the start point; jobless, penniless, homeless and lonely.

Since she descended from an East Afasinamean family, she thought of leaving for East Afasinamea hoping to get a job there. But as her nationality was West Afasinamean, it was impossible to be employed there. Then the IGA called her to their headquarters and offered to be their agent in West Afasinamea; in Hungupville namely, to report information they wanted about the NMB and about the official departments in general. As that was a dangerous and an illegal mission, she declined. Then the officer in charge smiled ironically and said, "Our citizens aren't cowards and it isn't a dangerous job. The information you may supply won't be used against the West but it will help us to build up an overall picture of the situation." "I couldn't be railroaded into a job I didn't want even though I had to starve." She turned her head away and murmured, "Oh! I wish I were married. All my efforts ended in failure." She lamented. When she declined, they expelled her from their country, just a few weeks before she got acquainted with Robert Dang whom she has been living with.

"I'm sorry, Jocelyn. You look frustrated and so sad. It seems what you're thinking of is dramatic." He sighed, thought a little and continued, "Well, Jocelyn, I need a graduate teacher terribly . . . ." Her face shone up and her eyes were filled with joy. "To teach whom? It should be your son!" She interrupted. His face reddened but he smiled shyly and said, "A tutor who can help us; my wife and I, in our online study. We need a degree whatever the price or the sacrifice is." "Then you're serious!" She said amazed. He nodded. She continued, "Well, I'll help both of you. Regardless of the open time I'll spend with you, I request a double salary of your secretary, Christina. We can start today. What do you say?" "Jocelyn, give me a chance to consult my wife and to think of your request. Here's my card. You can call me later. By the way, what's your cellular-phone number?" Joseph asked and handed her his card. She gave him the number and stood up placing her foot on the coffee table that all of the inner side of her other leg long and much higher showed up. "What about the date? Cancelled?" She asked signing with her hand to her makeup, her garments and her smooth hairless legs. He gave her a scornful look, smirked, and plunged his hand deep into his pocket, picked up a fifty-dollar bill and handed her. She gave a sigh of relief. "I think we'll sit together for long hours, many times. By the way, where do you live?" His question embarrassed her. It was unexpected. "I'm from Hungupville but Robert is from Lateburg. We were living in Hungupville but when Robert was unable to afford to the accommodation, we moved to Lateburg a few months ago." She answered. He stood up and so did she. They shook hands, kissed and she went out of his office.

Joseph rang Gillian and asked whether they can hire a tutor with a degree to help them in their studies. "A male or a female?" Gillian asked. "A female." Joe answered. She puffed and added, "Married?" "Her partner's a worker in the factory." He answered. "Joe, ask him if he can do a gardener. I won't have enough time for the garden. We'll give them the gardener's rooms to live in." She said. Joseph was very pleased. Strike while the iron is hot! He rang Jocelyn who was still waiting for a taxi at the factory gate. She hurried back to Joe's office, locked the door, threw her handbag on the carpet and threw herself between his arms.

On the contrary of his previous mood, minutes ago, he had a fierce lust for her. He hugged her that his arms were crushing her waist and his lips were smothering her. He lifted her on his arms and walked straight to the sofa. It was her life-time chance; the man and the job. Two birds with one stone. And his wallet in his pocket wouldn't be so far from her hand. He told her the good news in detail. She was floating in the air when he told her they could live in the gardener's rooms in his home garden. "Let's start today, Joe. The earlier, the better!" She said. "I'll send some people to have the place cleaned, well-furnished and suitable for my Venus." He said smiling. Her face shone with excitement. She pulled him to her breast. He hugged her again and lay down beside her on the too-narrow sofa for two people to lie on. She placed her head on his chest, her arm on his and her leg on his pelvis, dreaming. Then she rose up and lit a cigarette. Joe felt upset with the smoke. He coughed badly. She moved away and sat in the opposite seat, crossed her legs and gazed at Joe pleasantly.

Joe, too, was happy. Perhaps he felt happier than her. Less than a quarter of an hour, he ordered two cups of coffee. Christina; the executive secretary herself, brought a tray with two cups on. She was confused to see Jocelyn sitting in her seat as if she were a businesswoman. Jocelyn, with the strong woman's instinct felt that Christina was jealous. To drive her jealousy to madness, she addressed Joseph softly, "Joe, you aren't going to scrap in the last minute, are you?" Christina opened her eyes wide and murmured, "Joe?" Joseph, too, felt what the two women thought. He smiled mockingly giving Christina a side look and said, "Why should I? I need you definitely." Christina turned and headed to the door. She stumbled more than once in six steps. Jocelyn burst with laughter. When Christina slammed the door behind her, he smiled, shook his head and bent to turn his PC on. Jocelyn said, "Joe, why don't you use a lap top. It's modern and faster." Joseph answered that wherever he went there was a PC. Jocelyn didn't like that. She required a new lap top to prepare the lessons and to teach them.

Regardless of the fact that Joseph Miese was a successful businessman, he had never believed in insurance and his factory was a nonunion one. The inhabitants of Hungupville and Lateburg, too, who had known him, saw him as an example of ignorance and unintelligence. His employees, too, saw him as tightfisted and bad-mannered to everyone he might meet or talk to, but his mood indicated how wonderful he felt towards any educated people, especially women with degrees, regardless of their physique and their infamy. Over and above all, he was physically fortunate! There was something thrilling; something magnificent in his big body and something mocking in his dark eyes.

XI

Christina was a young woman, twenty-four years old. She was blond, medium-sized, shoulder-haired and with glasses. She had been reasonably proficient at her job as a successful executive secretary but she was a failure in love affairs. Her third boyfriend deserted her four months ago. Her colleagues in the secretarial office always referred to her as 'A Privet in the Field'. She had never taken any consideration to beauty salons or fashions. She always said that natural beauty was much important than the faked one.

Her father; Mr. Hydra, was a straight man but his obstinacy was proverbial. He was completely immovable when it came to scientific facts. He always consulted his lab or he went to his books to prove his right view point. So, he had never been defeated in any scientific field. To the romanticists and the naturalists, nature is beautiful; or rather it is the source of beauty.

Mr. Hydra was specialized in bio lab at the university; he was an insect researcher and he found beauty in insect eyes, proboscis, feelers, abdomen and wings. That was the natural beauty which wasn't deformed by the devastators; human beings. Christina was fond of her father and she was completely convinced with his opinion. She used to sit at the lab table for hours watching the smallest parts and organs of an insect or another through the microscope or under the magnifying lens, when she was a little girl. That love of the beauty of nature and that obstinacy passed from the father to his daughter. One thing Mr. Hydra didn't understand. It was that science beauty was different from romance and love beauty.

Christina had never considered insects as hateful creatures. She found beauty not only in butterflies and honey-bees, but also in Anopheles, mosquitoes in general, bugs, flies and cockroaches. She always said that the real beauty of things wasn't necessarily in the outer appearance only. Sometimes it was in the depth of things. She was right but she, too, forgot only a triviality. The beauty she was talking about was only in the scientific research. It's ironic that she didn't study biology at the university because she used to love insects and tiny organisms when she was a little girl.

An hour later, after she had brought the two cups of coffee to Jocelyn and Joseph, Christina was sure that Jocelyn had departed the factory. She herself rang a taxi for her. Therefore, she returned to the president's room with a sinister face and asked about Jocelyn's application. Mr. Miese automatically screwed his head round and looked at the top of the cabinet behind his chair. Then he looked at Christina questioningly. She said, "Sir, regardless of the fact that Jocelyn's story may sound convincing enough but in reality it's all complete eyewash. I had known her since I was a high-school girl. I, now and again, hear gossips about her misbehavior when she was a university student, a high school teacher and after. She was the most talked-about woman in Hungupville and Lateburg in the last decade.

Everyone knew in detail how she had been expelled from the university. Then she was a playful woman; she flirted with all male people she was working with. I heard when I was at college that Jocelyn was fired from the Education Department for her inefficiency. All knew the real grounds behind her resignation. She was a devil in a woman's dress. You signed a new secretary last week and so, you aren't going to appoint her in the overstaffed Secretarial Section, are you, Sir?" Although Joseph wasn't listening attentively to Christina, he spoke firmly, "Christina, go back to your office. Let me see my work! I'm the decision maker here." He was uncharacteristically acerbic in his tone. Christina turned back and left the president's office frowned.

Although there was a shared connection between Joseph and Christina; their loyalty to their work, there was still a long distance between them as a man and a woman. She was aware of that distance but she said it would never disturb her. Although Mr. Miese was extremely ignorant and harsh with others; arrogant and opinionated, he was unbelievably energetic. Christina was in her twenties, looking for love, and hungry for sex. Nevertheless, she used to say, "What an ass Joseph is!" She was only shaming as she always felt jealous when any woman talked to him; not to say smiled, laughed or winked at him. Unfortunately, her case was hopeless. Joseph's wife was a very beautiful woman and he was straight. Christina couldn't be a partner or a wife of him. Only one thing which wasn't less important than any serious relationship; it was casual love which would satisfy her hunger for sex. It was that Joseph had excessive energy and Christina had a long lasting hunger for making love. What she thought of was to help herself to be happier by satisfying herself sexually and to do Joseph a favor by giving him an outlet for his surplus energy. But that was too late. She couldn't understand male people; neither could she understand their instincts or desires. There was another woman taking care of Joe. She was Jocelyn. Joe would never think of Christina or lust after her because she looked like a man; a Privet in the Field! Those ideals made her offensive. She could have got rid of them if she wished.

A week later, Christina was at home watching a romance on TV. It reminded her of Jocelyn and Joseph. She remembered her colleagues in the accounting and secretarial sections and their comments and their remarks aiming at her. She also remembered her first boyfriend, Morris, leaving her for long, when she implored him, "You aren't going to desert me, Morris, are you? I love you. Please don't go! Morris! Morris! . . ." And she cried and many tears fell from her eyes then. She smirked and spat on the ground. She also remembered her second boyfriend and the third. They all wished she had changed. They said she was beautiful and that cosmetics and fashions would certainly emerge her beauty above one may fancy. She had closed her ears to all of what they had said.

In the weekend, she thought it was impossible to find all those people mistaken and her view point only was right. Therefore, she decided to try some make up.

Next Saturday afternoon, she went shopping alone. She bought face powder, lipstick, mascara, eye shadow, perfume, tweezers, a hairdryer, blue narrow jeans, a mini skirt and a lace deep V-collar blouse. To be fair, the collar reached the bottom of her breast parting. At home, she plucked her eyebrows, tried the new staff she bought and dressed her new top and the new skirt. Then she preened herself against the mirror in her bedroom. "Wooooow!" she shouted pleasantly. Then she changed and had the new narrow jeans on. She nodded and smiled. She felt sorry for all those days she wasted; she blamed herself. She hadn't understood her first friend. Any way, if she had, she wouldn't love him. She was a victim to his sweet but malicious tongue. The other two, although she didn't understand them either, they satisfied her sexually for some time.

She went to the kitchen where her mother was making tea. The old lady whistled and said, "Can I help you Princess?" She was amazed of her daughter's beauty. Christina dropped her head shyly, thanked her mother warmly, hurried to her with open arms and hugged her affectionately.

In Monday morning, she dressed, consulted her mirror for many minutes and went to the factory. Her colleagues; males and females, took her another woman when she was walking along the corridor into her office in the factory. All were amazed. Her female colleagues in the secretarial office whistled jealous; they were surprised. One of them said to her colleague who was sitting next to her, "Look! She's got promotion from Privet to Field Marshal!" Christina wasn't walking to her room then to her desk; she was sailing. She was a real princess.

Joseph Miese went into the secretarial office to ask Christina about some papers, but he saw another woman sitting at her desk. He turned to another secretary and asked whether Christina wasn't coming. They all laughed faintly. Christina coughed a little and said, "Yes, Sir!" Joseph was surprised. He didn't trust his eyes that he hushed dead. He gazed at her for a few seconds but he was unable to say anything. He only had his eyes as well as his mouth open wide for a moment. He forgot what he had come to the secretarial office for and so he turned back and left the room amazed.

His interest in Christina was so weak because he was married and later there was another woman, Jocelyn, who was amusing him. But now all conceptions turned upside down. Christina of today is absolutely different from Christina of last week and all the past weeks. Her sudden transformation implied that she was always a nice person but she didn't know nor did she want to know how to demonstrate her beautiful side.

XII

Jocelyn started to teach the Miese couple on the second day of her arrival to their house; to the rooms in the back garden. She used to sit in the recliner sofa in the study opposite to Joseph and next to Gillian. In the first evening, she was in her light blue hanky panky gown and an open robe on. Its large V-collar went down below the breast parting. In her open-cup bralette, she kept two cigarettes; one under each breast and a little lighter between them. On the second day, she wore shorts and a shirt with the three upper buttons undid. Later she was in an unstrapped dress covering a little of her breasts but nothing of her shoulders, her back or her legs. Her skirt was always micro mini, although she had a mini one once or twice and it was always with a side slit, which could be turned to be a front one. Over and above, she had the same perfume of Gillian! When they had their lesson online, she only moved a little in the recliner to give room to Joe to sit beside her opposite to the PC. Their close sides struggled to be acclimatized with the new pressure, although they had already been acclimatized since days. She was always between Joe and Gill, in the middle of the sofa recliner, and so Gillian always felt jealous and unrest.

Jocelyn said that the first lesson was going to be English Literature and History at the same time. She chose to introduce drama. She said they would like it and so they both felt happy. It was about the Greek dramatist Sophocles and his play *Oedipus Rex* which was a classic work. Joe and Gillian exchanged glances questioningly, but both were shy to ask what she meant by 'a classic work'. Joe asked about that writer Sophocles whether he had written that play before or after America was discovered. Jocelyn smiled scornfully and said that was long ago; before the New World was known. "New World? Are there more worlds than ours; the world we live in?" Gillian inquired and looked at Jocelyn sharply. There was a smirk on the teacher's lips although she made no comment. Then she added that Sophocles had written about King Oedipus although there were other kings in Greece at that time. Joseph was surprised. He asked whether Greece was larger than Australia to have many kings. Jocelyn felt disturbed. Without any comment, she went on reading and summarizing. She added that Greece then experienced the first democratic city-state in history but it had known tragedies only. "Why?" Gillian interrupted sadly and impatiently. "Were the Greeks so gloomy not to know what laughter was?" She asked. Jocelyn thought a little, then she said, "Don't you think the lesson will be too long and we'll waste much time if we keep on talking about the Greek literature, history and geography only?" Gillian nodded but Joseph kept silent. They both started to take notes and write a summary of what Jocelyn had said, but she neither add anything nor did she explain anything more. Suddenly, Gillian asked, "What was about that king (She looked down at her notebook.) Oedipus? Jocelyn smiled and said, "Let's have a short break for tea first. Then we'll continue."

Gillian rose up and walked to the kitchen. "Joe, don't you have a kiss for your sweetheart?" Jocelyn initiated. He extended his hands and his head to kiss her, but she retreated grabbing his hands and said, "Your wallet before your lips! I'm quite penniless!" When she saw his hand reaching his pocket, she jumped on him. He was waiting for such a sudden attack! Meanwhile, his left hand was in his back-pocket but his right one went down to soft spots of her body. Then they embraced and kissed affectionately. Although she was beastly thrilled, she said, "Stop it! That's enough, Joe. Stop it, please, or I'll take off my robe and my gown, too!" When Joe didn't listen to her, she pushed him back saying, "Gillian won't fire you out! She'll get back in a minute. Let's postpone it until later. I'll be waiting for you in the early morning."

She drew back to her place in the recliner, setting her hair and her clothing in order and inserting the hundred-dollar bill in her bra below her breast. Gillian returned with three glasses of tea and some biscuits on a tray. She put it on the coffee table and returned to her notebook. She took notice of Joseph. He breathed heavily. Then a side look at Jocelyn, but nothing looked unusual in her face or in her garments. She was still sitting in the same position she was in minutes ago. There was something unusual, but what was it? Joseph loved her and he was always loyal. "Is it the beginning?" She asked herself. Jocelyn picked two cigarettes from her bra; one for her and the other was for Joe. Joe shook his head and his hand; he didn't smoke. She returned one of the cigarettes into its hiding-place in the bra. Then she turned to Gillian, "Do you mind if I smoke?" Gillian didn't answer as she was preoccupied thinking of Joe. Jocelyn asked her again and patted on her shoulder. She had to repeat her question for the third time. "Sorry, Jocelyn! It harms me a lot. Could you go to the window, open it and smoke there, please?" The three of them were having their tea silently. Gillian was memorizing what she had just written. She was looking down at her notebook and up at the ceiling thoughtfully. She could hardly concentrate. It should be Jocelyn's nakedness. "She needs a good talking to, but how?" Gillian murmured. That should be embarrassing for both women. Then she decided that Joe had to. He hired her and so she should obey him.

When the three glasses were empty, Jocelyn held the tray and took it to the kitchen. "What's the matter, Joe? You look unstable!" Gillian asked. "Don't you see her outrageous clothes? If you were a man, you should be unstable, shouldn't you?" Joe said. Gillian nodded but she didn't say any word. When Jocelyn returned to her place in the recliner, she started, "Oedipus's father; the king, had a dream or a nightmare. It was that he'd have a son who'd kill him and marry his mother, the queen." "Oh! Oh! How horrible! How can one kill one's own child or one's dad and marry one's mom? Is it possible, Joe?" Gillian was shocked when she asked. Joe was amazed. But he was unable to answer. Then Jocelyn said, "It was only a dream; a nightmare as what I have just said. Well, it seems it's a hard lesson you have. You need an explanation pitched at a level suitable for young children! (Laughing) That's enough for this afternoon. We'll continue the lesson about Oedipus in the evening." "No, not this evening. Joe's taking me to have supper at the seashore." Gillian said. Then Jocelyn recommended they had better read the text online and she would continue the lesson next day afternoon. Nevertheless, she wished she had replaced Gillian at the seashore jaunt.

Late in the afternoon of the same day and before they drove to the seashore to have supper, the Miese couple read the play; *Oedipus Rex*, alone. Aside from the Greek names, they could tell it by heart.

In the second period, next day afternoon, when they came to the questions, all were shocked; the teacher as well as the Mieses. The first question was whether Oedipus Rex was a comedy or a tragedy. They all recognized it was a tragedy. The second question was about the differences between a tragedy and a comedy. Jocelyn said she would introduce a comedy soon and they would recognize the differences by themselves. The third question was whether it was written in verse or in prose. Jocelyn said literary sentences she remembered. They were incomprehensible to Gill or to Joe, but they were shy to ask. As Jocelyn was sure they didn't understand what she was talking about, although she herself couldn't tell what she was talking about. She said if they had been to a high school, they would have understood what she had said. If they did, they would find the material easier. Anyway, she promised she would answer all the questions, summarize and simplify the answers if they couldn't find them by themselves. She kept her promise on her own way.

In the next period, she introduced Sheridan's *School for Scandal*. She said it was a comedy and it was easy to find the difference between a comedy and a tragedy when they would have read it later. She wasn't interested in the third question! Neither the Mieses nor the teacher could tell why the third question wasn't answered. Had they all forgotten it?

Next week, she had to explain 'History of the English Language'. She had read online that the English Language was established in the second half of the Fourteenth Century. Joe didn't like the word 'established'. He looked at Gillian disturbed. "There was something mistaken. Can a language be established like a hospital, a university or a factory?" He wondered silently. "What did the English people speak before the second half of the Fourteenth Century?" Gillian asked aloud. Eventually, they dared to ask Jocelyn. She was evasive when she was asked questions she was unable to answer. She said they had better check the answers by themselves online. "People and students study and learn alone by themselves. Teachers only help and organize." She said. She was very ingenious in finding excuses.

After two weeks, Gillian complained they wouldn't finish on that rate. Jocelyn answered that they wouldn't be able to understand everything well if she went on introducing the whole lesson at one time. Each lesson would take long hours. Then she said when she was a university student, they needed a week for what the Mieses had on one day, and that English and History were so difficult to study or learn out of the university.

XIII

On May Day and upon Gillian's recommendation, the Mieses decided to invite the factory employees and laborers; single or married, to their country house at the river side, not far from the lake. The Dangs, the chauffeur and his wife could come, too. As it was on Saturday, they had to confirm their coming on Friday noon. They could go on Saturday and spend the night there. There was enough room for all of them. Mr. Miese was going to pitch tents at the edge of the forest in addition to the two stories of his own house. The number of tents would depend upon the number of the attendants; how many people would be present. The total number of the factory employees and laborers was eighteen. Six of them were married; twelve were single, in addition to the Dangs, the chauffeur and his wife and the Mieses themselves. They all confirmed they would be at the Miese's country house between Saturday noon and sunset. The general manager didn't. He apologized because his wife was seriously ill. They hoped it would be clear and warm. Otherwise there would be no barbecue, no swimming, and no lying in the dark shades of the forest trees. None would wrap the beloved neck or waist with their arms while walking along the track at the river side. There would be meals, barbecue, meat, seafood, pastry and dessert, fruit, drinks of all kinds for the afters. There would be dance, fun, boat-riding, fishing, roaming in the forest and sitting and walking in the house front and back gardens which were as large as a football playground. Luckily, the weather was set fair for vacation. It was a warm spring day exactly as it came in the weather forecast which wasn't always reliable.

Jocelyn told The Miese couple that she would surprise them on May Day but she asked them to allow her to go to their country house earlier than the others in Saturday morning. When Gillian said that she would tell the chauffeur to take her to the country house but she wanted to know what was behind her demand. Joseph was listening silently and he was surprised of such an unexpected request. She smiled and said, "I'm a good archer. I was trained when I was a high school girl to represent a Roman warrior in a historical play. I can hunt wild boar, buffalo calves, stags, pigeons, bustards, coots, francolins and grouse. You needn't buy meat or poultry of any kind." Gillian and Joseph didn't believe their ears. When Joseph shook his head doubtfully, she said, "If I don't hunt enough animals and birds for the party, you can fire me. But if I could, what would my reward be?" "Five hundred dollars! But have you got a bow and arrows?" Gillian asked.

When Joseph didn't hear an immediate answer from Jocelyn, he said, "I'll buy them in an hour but you've to train us how to use a bow and how to shoot arrows. Deal?" "Deal!" Jocelyn said joyfully. On his way out to buy what she required, he asked her, "How many arrows do you want?" "Three in a quiver, please. Only three!" Jocelyn said. Joseph nodded and went out. In a few seconds, he turned back. The two women looked at him questioningly. "But it isn't allowed to catch or hunt birds and wild animals." Joseph said. "That isn't on May Day or on The Easter!" Jocelyn said. He shrugged and went out.

The country house; the light green house, which was refurbished a week ago, was set on the hillside surrounded by thick, high and dark green trees. The massive and thick olive trees hugged the house delightfully with their umbrella-shaped branches over the roof. They protected the house from the hot sun in summer and they formed a safe and quiet place for many kinds of birds to sing in the early morning and at sunset, to have a snooze at noon, to sleep at night and to nest in the spring. The shade was cool even in the three burning months; June, July and August. Once one could go there, one would long to turn back again and again.

Eleanor had to stop working for the Mieses more than nine years ago. Only a few months after she had been fired, she was the closest friend of Cecil Pearce, three years older than her. Cecil was a surveyor, living and working in Lateburg as well as Eleanor. They had been in love for a couple of years before they married. She was an orphan, and she married the man she loved. None had the right to ask, accept, reject or oppose. Her expectation and her estimation to Cecil were absolutely right that she had never resented her marriage and she was a marvelous housewife later. Cecil was really in love with her. She was his first love; and unfortunately his last! She always said that he loved her much more than she did although she absolutely adored him. They shared everything; from laughter to tears for almost six years. They had their daughter Mattie six years ago. Cecil loved life and he was successful in his work.

For a higher salary and better work conditions, he resigned and volunteered in the army. Two years later, his regiment had to move to Asia as auxiliaries. West Afasinamea's Super-Power ally was warring against a ruthless military dictator who oppressed his people and threatened his democratic and peaceful neighbors. Many of the opposition men were executed including citizens of that Super-Power country as a result of that tyrant oppression. Cecil wasn't desirous to leave his home, his beloved wife, his kind mother and his little daughter Mattie but his leaders told him he had to serve his country abroad and he had to abide by the regulations.

When Cecil told his wife Eleanor he was moving with his regiment to Asia, she had a strong feeling that he wasn't getting back. She implored him, "If you're gone, all interests of life will be worthless. All elations will be spoiled." Cecil, the soldier, had to value honor above life and leave with his unit to Asia. Otherwise he would face a long imprisonment.

Cecil left with his military companions for a country they had known on the map only. With that sorrowful farewell of Cecil, all those could make a diversion in Eleanor's life died away. Nevertheless, he used to contact them by phone and by Internet communication means when he had the chance to do and that comforted them a little. He also sent Eleanor and Mattie presents twice. He longed above all else to see his family again. He was getting back on vacation or for long in six months from his departure, but death was impatient and faster. After four months, the army told Eleanor, his wife, and Mrs Diana Pearce, his mother, in two letters but simultaneously that Cecil was killed.

Since her husband's death, she had abandoned herself to despair. She lamented, "I can't imagine going through life without him." She had been in black and she refused to face the fact that death was common and certain. People lived and thought differently but death didn't change; heart and brain got at rest and that was all. It was always the same. Then ordinary poor people equated with the elite members in the eyes of death; although it is blind!

Seven months ago, Eleanor started a privet school of her own. The school was small and it included the first three levels for young children. The staff was all women, generally married and older than her. They felt the tragedy of Eleanor and they were really sorry for her. Therefore, they planned to help her forget her calamity and live a normal life. Marion was the eldest of them, and so she was the first to talk to Eleanor. "Come on, Eleanor! It's certain we'll love those handsome youths who love us and they won't hesitate to make us happy! You won't find it easy at the beginning, but everything passes with time. Time will heal all, as it's said, and the image will faint away from memory. You're sweet and youth. You need not a long time to fall in love again. Women like you are well sought. Men of taste and morals don't leave us in peace very long after they get here. (She pointed at her heart and her colleagues burst with laughter.) You want food, water and air to live, don't you? Yes, you do. So you want a fine man! A fine man to please you! Let's enjoy this short life, Eleanor! It isn't the life we aspire, but we've to live it. You're young, dear. Regardless of how a woman of culture and of education you're, you'll never imagine how you'd feel when you're older (Marion patted on her chest.) Life quickens. It doesn't wait for us! We're unable to

fight fate but we've to make advantage of every new day."
Marion, Eleanor's colleague, said enthusiastically. Eleanor
was listening silently. Her voice choked but self-esteem made
her face flush with obstinate tears determining to fall down
when she tried to say something. She nodded, rose up and
left the room quickly before tears track on her cheeks. There
was much praise and encouragement. It was evident that
Eleanor's colleagues were eagerly pleased to see her happy.

On another day, Eleanor-school teachers winked at
Louisa to talk to her. Although Louisa couldn't match
up Marion in conversation, she addressed Eleanor, "You
listened carefully to Saint Marion last time." They all roared
with laughter including Marion herself and Eleanor. Then
Louisa added, "Could you listen to me?" Eleanor nodded.
"Good! Look Eleanor! I know how your life's important
to you. So is love! If I were you, although your situation is
much better than mine! Your husband's dead and he's really
dead. We must all die sometime. We can't fight nature, or
destiny. That's just a fact of life. But my husband's dead
although he's alive!" They burst with laughter when Louisa
said her last word in her Louisan tone! "If I were you, I'd try
to dig up joy wherever and whenever I could! We've to live
our real life; not to persist on the life we imagine exactly.
It doesn't last forever and so we don't have enough time to
waste thinking about the dear people we miss. What I'm
sure of is that time will make you feel better. A vacation will
do you a power of good. Go out of your dark prison! Go
out on the razzle. Go and enjoy yourself in clubs and bars.
Climb mountains and hills. Sit on their tops. Sit by rivers, by
lakes and by the sea. Have a look at the sun at day and when
the moon and the stars glitter at night; only for a change."

Louisa concluded. "The world would look pitiful without Louisa's playful puns and her clever remarks!" Olivia said laughing, stroking Louisa's cheek with gentle fingers.

There was a demonstration in Lateburg. Families, from Hungupville and Lateburg, of those who were killed in wars abroad were demonstrating against war. In fact, the opposition organized demonstrations in the whole country. When the government broadcast on all organs of public opinion and at the Nineteenth-Hour News on Thursday the Twenty-ninth of April about official celebrities on May Day and that the Representatives together with the Cabinet Members would held a meeting in The House on the second day; Friday the Thirtieth of April, the Opposition took advantage of the occasion. They called for an antiwar demonstration in the capital only. They wanted it to be a unique, expressive and convincing. It should be broadcast live on all TV nets, news agencies and radio stations. They would succeed to arouse the nation's sympathy as their slogans would be reasonable and national. They would absolutely raise the devil.

Sixteen dozen of university female students from the capital universities followed by orphans and widows of war victims would lead the demonstration which would surround The House of Representatives at the time of the meeting. The orphans would be in blue, the widows in black and the girl students in bikinis! Each two dozen would be in colored bikini sets different from the other dozen. The first two dozen were in blue bikinis. Their banner read: PLEASE MAN OF PEACE: Their placards were: DISBAND THE ARMY! NO MORE WARS! NO MORE BLOODSHED! NO MORE AIR BASES!

REINFORCE THE POLICE! The red bikinis' banner read: WAR AGAINST: And their placards were: POVERTY! DISEASE! UNEMPLOYMENT! IGNORANCE! CORRUPTION! INFLATION! ORGANIZED CRIME! DRUGS! SMUGGLING! The third banner of the yellow bikinis read: FREE! And the placards were: EDUCATION! MEDICATION! TRANSPORTATION! HOUSING! SOCIAL SECURITY! The fourth banner read: WE WANT MORE! And their placards were: SCHOOLS! UNIVERSITIES! SCIENTIFIC REASERARCH CENTERS! HOSPITALS! INDUSTRIES! FACTORIES! DAMS! INFRASTRUCTURE! JOBS! The last banner; the eighth, was the most effective one. It was: I LOVE YOU! I ELECTED YOU! LOVE ME! LOVE YOUR COUNTRY! DO A LITTLE FOR OUR OWN INTEREST!

The Representatives together with the Secretaries (Ministers) heard feminine angry and noisy shouts outside the meeting hall. They felt disturbed and they were curios. The chairman was unable to control the meeting. Therefore, he rang his bell for a ten-minute break. Representatives and Secretaries hurried to the windows and to the balconies of the meeting hall. Crowds of people were blaring out the drums behind rows of bikini girls. To read the banners, the placards and to peer at bikini maps which were the most important, some of the Representatives and Secretaries had to peer at them over their glasses. Others got their little binoculars from their pockets and gazed at the almost naked girls. A bald member covered his head with a cartable and others set their ties, smoothed down their hair and waved with their hands. They dribbled over their robes and they licked their lips.

After the ten-minute break, the chairman rang his bell once, twice and three times in vain. None had the intent to hear that shy and inconvenient bell; none was desirous to leave his place and go back to his seat in the hall. Then a strong voice from a loudspeaker announced a surprise! "Good news! Our super powerful friend-country president will grant each of you a million dollars when the new marine and air base motion passes." They didn't wait to return to their seats; they lifted their hands 'In Favor' when they were still on the balconies and at the windows. The motion was passed with one accord. Even the Opposition Representatives voted 'In favor' of the motion flagrantly.

As the meeting was broadcast live, demonstrators poured out of their homes leaving what they were doing and wandered the streets of all towns in the country including Lateburg, protesting against the award! The Prime Minister, in a short word which was broadcast live, said laughing that he wished he had been able to grant every citizen a million dollars.

The National Party was nicknamed 'The Four Us' / juːz/ by the press and the mob. It was a nickname formed from the initials of their letters' subject addressed to the elite members: Unavoidable Ultimatum to Unpatriotic Usurpers. It was an opposing party. Its members inside and outside The House had their video cameras and their mobile cams to take pictures of the attendants on the hall balconies and the crowds in the streets as well. Since they have members who were reporters and observers all over the country, they depended upon scandal to achieve their goals. As it was well known that many politicians and decision makers were not always far from scandal, they recorded every movement and every word of the elite members. Politicians everywhere were always accused of hypocrisy and mendacity.

When the Secretary of Foreign Trade went back home, he opened his mail box to find an unstamped envelop. When he opened it, there were three pictures enclosed. One of them was his own photo when he was blowing a kiss to one of the bikini girls. The second was the girl herself blowing him a kiss. And the third was fabricated that it joined them together with a little note: 'Congratulation! She loves you! You Love her! What about Mary? What does she like? Thank you for half of the prize! A courier will be waiting at your home door tomorrow at noon sharp!' His face whitened. When he got into his home, his wife, Mary, was waiting for him in a light dress and heavy makeup! She gave up hope of any pleasure when she saw him depressed and so she went to the bathroom washed her face and got back to the bedroom and changed!

The Four Us had observed Joseph Miese and his successful work. They sent him a letter telling him that he had to pay two-hundred and sixty-five thousand dollars in taxes for that year only. They asked him to pay them only one million dollars and they would cover him for ten years to come, during which he wouldn't pay a penny.

Joseph went to the Inter-Tax Department and they assured him that he would pay that amount of money. He consulted his accountant who said that the tax should be paid or he might be imprisoned. Then Joseph called the Four-Us headquarters and told them he was paying half a million dollars to their charities and he would pay a similar amount next year. The member of the Four-Us who answered the phone told Joseph that the one-million-dollar should be one payment and it was nonrefundable but if he paid them two million, it would be refundable completely; two million dollars, after ten years. Joseph apologized for lack of liquidity and said he would get a loan from the bank to pay one million dollars only. They accepted and they intimidated him into silence.

The National Party or The Four Us was suspected to be a tool in the hands of East-Afasinamea leadership as the majority of its members descended from the East when the two Afasinameas were one united country. Although the press, the police and the intelligence-service men tried hard to catch them red-handed, their attempts failed.

The official authorities celebrate each year on May Day all over the country. With the patronage of the two municipalities of Hungupville and Lateburg, celebration in that area could take place. As Hungupville was a hilly town and Lateburg was flat, the two municipalities agreed that the celebration should take place yearly in Lateburg whose municipality had to put on the celebration but Hungupville municipality financed and supervised it. There were fireworks, music, dance and a majestic parade. Showers of jasmines, daffodils and flowers always fell over the parade participants from windows and upper stories in Lateburg. Groups of children in coloured costumes marched in rows and lines. The municipal band, in uniform, was playing harmonious and merrily tunes. Groups of folklore from the whole area took share in the celebration. Some danced, some others sang and others performed short comedies.

Lateburg Mayor insisted on that Eleanor's school children should have a share in the procession. He was so happy to see his only grandson marching in his costume with his school mates in the Main Street of his town. Eleanor, as a widow of a victim of war, had to join the opposition in their demonstration. She was unable to take an absolute decision. Her colleagues recommended that she should share in the demonstration on the first day and in May-Day celebrity on the second day and so both sides; the authorities and the opposition, would be content. Eleanor smiled and nodded. She participated in the opposition demonstration. When the Lord Mayor of Lateburg saw her, he smiled and encouraged her. She felt pleased and gave a sigh of relief.

Eleanor and her colleagues had to accompany the children and to keep them in order and safe in the May-Day celebrity. Miss Olivia was in front of the children and Eleanor was behind them.

On their way to their country house, the Mieses had to go along the Main Street in Lateburg. As the traffic had to detour to alternative routes or it had to wait until the celebration finished, the Mieses preferred to wait and watch the parade. To their amazement, Eleanor was marching behind a group of little children. The Mieses waved to her. When she took notice of them, she laughed and answered their greeting that she waved her hands enthusiastically, giving them a sign to wait for her. Half an hour later when the parade arrived at the Municipality Square and after the National Anthem was played, the Mayer spoke to the celebrators before they returned home.

Gillian remembered that they had to buy a cartoon of mineral water for Matt and at the same time they had to wait for Eleanor. Therefore, Gillian and Matt went to the Square on foot leaving Joe in the car to buy the water when the stores would reopen normally. In a quarter of an hour, the Mayor finished his word. Then Eleanor gathered her school children in their bus and gave the teachers and the driver strict instructions to send them to their homes. Eleanor always took great pains to ensure the safety of_her school children. Then she clasped her daughter in her hand and went back in the same street to meet the Mieses. She walked only a hundred yards when she met Gillian and Matt. She welcomed them with open arms. They embraced and laughed. Gillian was happy to meet Eleanor again, but Eleanor was happier. Matt was the happiest to meet his favorite and his first teacher after nine-year parting. Gillian and her son were extremely happy to find out that Eleanor had married and she had a child. But she was in black and there was a sign of sadness on her face which was without any kind of makeup.

Gillian had known that Eleanor was an orphan; therefore it couldn't be one of her parents died recently. Could it be a brother or a sister? But Eleanor was the only child of her parents. Then a shocking idea flashed in her brain. It would be extremely sorrowful if it were her husband. She was still young! Gillian felt sorry for Eleanor but she was embarrassed to ask her about those black clothes.

Joe came in his car and stopped next to them. He shook hands with Eleanor and they embraced. He got notice of her sad face and her black clothes from the first while. As his manners were appalling, one couldn't take him anywhere. He impatiently asked what the matter was with her. Her eyes were filled with tears, so she dropped her head and said it was her husband. He was killed in Asia a year ago. She wiped her eyes and blew her nose. When they asked her how and when that happened, she said, "I looked into the story they told me, and I found out it was perfectly true. His friends in his unit told me they had seen Cecil walking with a boy and they were talking amiably. That Asian boy told Cecil that his lost friend, Privet Dane, was locked in a deserted house not far from his location. He could free him easily if he wished and he demanded ten dollars to lead him to the place and a reward when he had him freed. The boy looked terrified and he implored Cecil not to tell anyone. Otherwise, he would be executed. Cecil believed him that he didn't tell anyone of his companions where he was going. He risked his life to rescue his friend. He thought it would take him only a couple of minutes and he would return with Dane safe. On his way to the place where Dane was supposed to be, he was shot on his head. The boy threw the ten-dollar bill on his chest. At first we thought he'd been kidnapped but later it turned out that he'd been deceived, and gone with that boy of his own will. When that boy was captured, he confessed his conspiracy with the killers, 'I had to defend my country against the attackers who menaced it on my own way.' He said boldly. When one of the officers said that Cecil was one of the saviours who came to free them of the dictatorial junta and of the tyrant oppression, he said whom they called tyrant was his uncle. Both of them belonged to the same tribe and that the invaders, our men, knew nothing about their culture and about their community. How sorrowful and painful it was! That was a year ago; a year in which I suffered a lot." Then she raised her head up smiling, although tears were still in her eyes, and asked Joe teasingly whether Hungupville was still an independent republic; with a hint to her work with them more than nine years ago. Joseph smiled shyly and said, "That was yesterday; and yesterday was another day. Hungupville had changed a lot since then."

Then Joe told her they were having guests down from the factory on May Day. She could be included in that invitation. "Each of our invitations is designed to entertain and surprise our guests; leaving them always anxious to come back." Joe said teasingly. Gill and Matt reassured the invitation. They said she could come today as it was Saturday and spend the night with them. "I'd love to. I've recognized much about the beauty of the place. I had once spent a pleasant day in the country with Cecil." Eleanor said and sighed. A tear dropped from her eye.

She was longing to meet them. All those years, she couldn't forget how happy she had been with them. She had the intention and the determination to call at Gillian's and to see her and her son Matt, but her pride and her dignity prevented her. When the invitation was reassured, Eleanor thought long. "Everybody's giving me a piece of advice, and it sounds reasonable." She murmured. Then the melodious voice of Gillian came, "We'll be so pleased with your company. One could sleep in the afternoon, if the heat were excessive. Over and above, we have a surprise for you." Eleanor contemplated the dark times of the past year, with the days going unchanged. She felt she was throttled. Agonies and memories haunted her head that she cried and tracks of tears were drawn on her cheeks. Then she decided she had to go out. It was her first vacation alone; without Cecil. "I'd love to as I have nothing on tomorrow, but what I dislike is the trouble that may spring from my staying there." Eleanor said. "Forget all these illusions. It would be a nice spring evening. I know you need to recover and it would be a blessing to have you around. You'll tell your friends about your wonderful experiences on the weekend of the year! It will be as you want it to be or even better. Don't miss it!" Gillian asserted with a wink.

Despite the obstinate tears in her eyes, an earnest and strange feeling of peace and joy fell upon her suddenly. She had recognized well it was impossible to prophesy the future with any extent of truthfulness; whether it could be as beautiful and pleasing as the past. Anyway, she took the decision that the course of her life should be changed. As far as one lives, one changes. So does life. It should be variable. She wouldn't be a widow forever living upon her dead husband's memory. She would stop abandoning herself to despair. Eventually, she decided to go to the beauty salon and to dress in fashion. "I must make myself presentable in the guests' eyes." She thought. She wanted to attract the attendants' attention in general, and the senior employees who were bachelors in particular. They should be educated with degrees, of high salaries and handsome. Nevertheless, she wasn't going to be a plotter girl and steal the other girls' men. She hoped she would like the visitors there as she always liked the common people, the labourers and the employees. She always felt she was at home among them. Finally, she nodded and said, "Do you think I ought to bring anything with me?" Gillian shook her head. They all felt happy. They would send her the chauffeur in an hour. Eleanor thought a little and said that three hours would give her a better chance to join them. They all agreed. Then they got her cellular phone number and went on their way to their country house.

The Mieses arrived at their country house earlier than the others but Jocelyn with the two workers, whom Joseph had hired last Friday, had arrived at the house since four hours, and they were hunting in the neighboring forest. Factually, Jocelyn went hunting alone. She told the two workers that it would be noisy and that the birds and the animals would fling away if they hear, see or smell them. Therefore, they had to wait for her at the forest boundary until she returned. In less than three hours, Jocelyn with the two men returned with eleven different large birds, six hares and a small stag in a wheel barrow. The two chefs and the servers hurried with the hunt to the kitchen. The stag, hares and birds offal and some of their soft flesh was to be fried and roasted for supper. "In the early morning, tomorrow, I'll do my best to hunt a calf and one boar at least. Then I'll go to the river for fishing! Oh, no. I won't go fishing tomorrow; I'll go today afternoon." Jocelyn said boasting.

"Will you go fishing with a bow and arrow?" Gillian asked amazed. "Yes, I will. To catch a large fish with an arrow is easier than hunting a hare with the same weapon!" She added.

Late in the afternoon, Jocelyn went alone with her bow and two arrows for fishing in the river and in the neighboring lake; the third arrow was broken in the morning when she was hunting in the forest. The lake, as well as the river, was only three hundred yards from the Miese's country house. After about an hour, Jocelyn returned with nine large fish. The guests, who had arrived at the Miese's country house, together with the hosts praised her much lauded work.

The Mieses stood at the gate out to greet the other guests. The guard and the servers welcomed them; they waved their hands and said a quick hello. As it was warm and clear, they sat in the garden having light drinks, talking, joking and laughing when they heard china clicking. It was seven sharp and it was time for supper. Tables were set with all kinds of food and drinks. The servers stood in the hall. "I hope the supper is to your liking!" Gillian said smiling pleasantly.

Eleanor sent her daughter Mattie to her grandmother Mrs. Diana Pearce and went to the beauty salon. They both always liked to be together. Mattie was fond of her grandma that she liked to spend the night and every night with her.

Mrs. Miese sent the chauffeur to Lateburg to Eleanor. When he rang her a little before sunset, she had just come from the beauty salon and was waiting for him. She enjoyed the drive along that narrow, winding upward and downward track in the hilly area in the country with woods, farms, orchards and vineyards at the two sides. The house emerged when they were half a mile away. It was ablaze with dazzling lights that it looked as if it were noon on a sunny day although the sun had already set.

XIV

Eleanor came into the Mieses' country house when the guests were having supper. The chauffeur rang Mrs. Miese when he was parking the car just round the corner from the gate. She received Eleanor at the front door of the house and led her to Matt's table in his room upon his request and she told her, "Your room will be up there to give you some privacy. Our room's at the other side; opposite to yours. (Biting her thumb and thinking) Did you bring any clothes appropriate for vacation?" Eleanor nodded and smiled. Gillian answered the smile, left them and went back to her guests in the dining room.

Matt had been very sad and he had complained her sudden departure without giving him a 'Bye, bye'. He was sitting at the table silent, chewing his food so slowly and giving her hesitative looks. "What's the matter, Matt? Anything wrong?" Eleanor asked. As he felt that Eleanor was a sister of his, and that was what they both really felt, Matt said, "Do you mind if I ask you a question?" "Right, fire away! You aren't waiting for my permission, are you?" "Why did you leave me so abruptly without a farewell?" He asked crying and hiding his face on her shoulder. She was patting on his back when she said she wished she could but her sudden departure was unexpected and that was beyond her will. Anyway, both of Eleanor and Matt were very happy to sit at the same table alone. His face shone up. He told her he was doing well at school and he was taking his finals in a couple of months. Then he added, "And what do you do now?" When she looked at him amazed, he remembered, nodded his head, smiled a little and said, "A school teacher, aren't you?" She said she had started a small privet school of her own since seven months. Then she added, "Did it ever occur to you that I loved you heartily, truly with all my senses and my emotions? I loved you for years before I finally met you again. Because I loved you, I called my little daughter Mattie after you and I started my school for young children like you (She smacked her forehead). Sorry, I mean who are at the same age you had been when I knew you." Matt, too, smiled and his eyes glittered with joy. Eleanor was talking as if she were his older sister.

Eleanor and Matt were eating and talking and so they sat for a long time at the table.

When the guests finished supper, they moved individuals and couples to the sinks between the kitchen and the bathrooms. They had to pass by Matt's room which was ajar. Jocelyn glimpsed a woman at Matt's table. She looked like Eleanor; an old acquaintance of Jocelyn, but she wasn't sure. She couldn't trust her eyes and dismissed the idea from her mind. When she was drying her hands with some tissues, it occurred to her that it would do no harm if she looked inside the room again. She was taken aback when she recognized her. Jocelyn had never known that the Mieses had ever made any acquaintance with Eleanor. Her heart began drumming. It was a blow fell unexpectedly. Since Eleanor was at Matt's table alone, then she had been one of the Mieses' close friends. The joy on Jocelyn's face fainted out. Her spirits dropped dramatically. "We've had it!" She murmured. Her plans would never succeed if Eleanor spoke. She shouldn't see her. Jocelyn should be careful.

After supper, the guests dispersed everywhere; inside the house, in the gardens and even outside the Miese's estate; along the track at the river side and in the forest. Jocelyn went to Clement who was sitting and leaning up against a rock in Mr. Miese's back garden with a bottle of wine in his hand. She sat beside him. He initiated her, "I'm sorry for you; sorry to see you throwing away happiness with your own hands; trying to get something that would never make you happy and I keep on running astray. You don't like that, do you? You've suffered a lot in the past years for a husband." "The blind's leading the lame!" She commented with a scornful smile. Then she added, "Patience, dear! My plan is being put into action."

She was certain without a faint doubt that she would get advantages from the Mieses' unawareness. "What about Paul?" Clement asked her interestingly. "He wants a woman with a good job and a high degree." She answered sorrowfully. "I will make him pay for the battering he gave me!" "But he was your closest friend. He was a good man, anyway. Why can't you trust me? I will make my sweetheart Jocelyn a splendid husband when your plans succeed!" Clement said and rested his aching head on her shoulder. He didn't even know what plans she had. Jocelyn's heart was filled with joy. She was certainly the happiest woman in the world. He was the first man, may be the only one who had ever made her such an offer.

It was very obvious that Clement was physically exhausted. Nevertheless, he looked at her as if she were a prey as the worm to the little bird. What would he do or say if her plans didn't succeed? "But this isn't the place. You might ask your kind hostess to allow me wait in one of the rooms. The house looks big." He implored. "Mrs. Miese doesn't know me." He added "But she knows me and I don't want her to acquaint with you!" Jocelyn answered unpleasantly. He laughed hysterically that his sides were shaking and the tears flowed down on his cheeks. Jocelyn said amazed, "Hush!" she was alarmed as he laughed aloud, "The walls have ears in the Miese's tonight." She didn't even ask him why he was laughing although he was extremely tired! Her joy and her happiness blinded her. Then her happiness, her cheek blush and her joy all died out when she heard a faint voice getting nearer to their place. She whispered horrified, imploring him to hush and closed his mouth with her hand. He wasn't physically tired; he was drunk.

It was Robert Dang and a taxi driver. She always told Robert where she was and when she was turning back. Robert had also strict instructions of what to do in emergency. When the taxi driver winked at her, she paid him off with money from Joe's wallet and said, "We must lose no more time. You should take him home! He'll spoil all our plans." Clement went with the taxi driver. Then she turned to Robert and said, "And you too, get into the house!" He obeyed her without any further comment. "Have no fear for me!" She added. He went to the door of their assigned room and listened. She followed him but she diverged to the left and sat in a seat in the drawing room. There were only a few people in that room. A few minutes later, she left the room and got out of the house to talk to somebody in a shady corner in the back garden.

Michael had never made love with Christina, yet she knew he loved her. She couldn't be mistaken about it. She felt that by her inner mind as he always made eyes at her. Too often she caught sight of him looking at her with yearning and that puzzled her. Why hadn't he told her yet? That was what she couldn't understand. He was always courteous, but he was cold and unapproachable.

Christina's sight to the real life had changed differently. She had positively changed one hundred and eighty degrees for the better. She stood opposite to her mirror and patted her smooth shoulder hair satisfactorily. The white skin and her large green eyes with the makeup on her face emerged her beauty and raised her spirits. She smiled and her eyes were filled with joy to see her dimples showing out so pleasantly. "Natural beauty! Huh! What crazy I was!" She laughed while she was talking to her image in the mirror. "Michael will be mad. Yes, I will send him mad. It's Christina the Second. Christina the First died." She added enthusiastically.

When Christina arrived at the Mieses' country house, all heads and eyes were raised up towards her. She was a real beauty. Michael was freshly barbered, shaved and massaged and he was holding her hand between his affectionately. He was completely obsessed with her. She had the intention, the plan and the determination not to lose him, even after her back had bent and her hair had silvered. She could only keep him if she understood him; and she certainly would.

Michael was also a graduate. He was her colleague in the Miese's factory and he was four years older than her. He was handsome, wiry and single. Michael and Christina used to meet in offices as he was an accountant and she was an executive secretary in the same factory. They used to exchange a word, or to discuss something concerning their work. Both had a watchful eye on the other. Michael had never crossed the borders of fellowship with her, so she hadn't. His bold dark eyes always laughed at her. When she changed her opinion with the true natural beauty, they both came closer and closer to each other. They loved each other for love. Her love was of a young girl for a man she hadn't yet understood well, a man who owned all the traits she missed.

"Would Christina join the party?" Jocelyn wondered in Saturday morning. When they met in the Miese's country house, she was shocked to see Christina had changed from top to bottom but to the better. She was so beautiful and attractive with a handsome guy. Jocelyn, herself, with her beauty and her makeup, had never dreamed of such a boyfriend, even in her early university days, more than ten years ago. The guests' eyes looked at Christina hungrily. They would eat her if they could. Christina liked their gazing and so she whispered to Michael who, too, was gazing at her lovingly; completely obsessed with her, "How wonderful these people are! I'll never forget how nice this day is till the last breath in my life." Then she talked to herself, "This night, this hour, I have to tell Michael what I feel and what I think of."

When she shared him a dance, and her face was against his ear and she was going to acknowledge her love and to announce it, he said softly and affectionately, "I love you, Christina. I've loved you for months before I finally befriended you. I loved you but I didn't want you know it. You were so brutal and obstinate to all those who loved you. (Her arms wrapped his neck firmly.) If you listen for a few minutes I'll explain everything." But she couldn't. Her lips stuck to his and she kissed him affectionately. They were so attached to each other.

Joe came into Matt's room as a host to exchange a word with Eleanor as a kind of hospitality. He sat at the same table with them. After a few words, Matt left the room closing the door behind him. They both kept silent. Joe was looking at her speculatively. His unstable eyes examined her from tiptoes up to her waist and over to her forehead. On his face there wasn't any trace of sorrow or pain, but passions only. Although dead, they were trying to stir. He was proud enough to fancy Eleanor saying, 'I was, am, will be always your little girl! I was thrilled when I saw you.' And that she would bury her head upon his chest. He had the feeling that she amused him more than anything else in the world. 'I'm not going to lose you again. And if I lost you, nothing else mattered. Neither friends nor money nor anything.' She would say. He had the intent to pursuit some kind of relationship with her and that her thoughts should be the same as they had been before. Although widowed, she was fascinating as if she were a single young girl. She was happy now, only because she met him. A few hours ago, when he saw her in the street, she had been miserable. He completely forgot what she had told him before.

Eleanor rose up and walked to the window for fresh air. Joe followed her. She looked over her shoulder to find him exactly behind her and so she was terrified. Then he put his hands fiercely upon her and pinned her shoulders to the wall. She commanded aloud, "Take your hands off me! Let me go! I warn you! Gillian's my friend. I won't cheat her." "But Jocelyn says there'd be no remorse at loving another woman's husband." Joseph said. "Then go to your Jocelyn! Although I don't know her, she seems of no dignity to lose." Eleanor concluded. Although she had strong hunger for sex, she refused to respond positively. Then she clenched her teeth and added scornfully, "You have to forget me forever, and what happened in Hungupville nine years ago was in the past and that past's dead." He took his hands off her and apologized saying, "I'm sorry, Eleanor. I had no intention to hurt your feelings." He turned back and left the room.

When Matt returned, he noticed Eleanor upset. He thought a little, and then he said, "Would you like to take a round in the garden. It's warm outside?" "Do you have any pets here?" Eleanor asked. "Yes. We've a tank of colored freshwater fish; namely Goldfish and Beta fish and we also have two nice dogs." Matt answered. "Good! Pets can reduce the amount of stress in one's life. Let's go and see them." Eleanor said and they both got out. As the lights were timed to put out one each half an hour, lighting wasn't so dazzling as before but it was pretty acceptable.

Eleanor and Matt walked in the garden and round the house. Matt showed her the tulip plants he planted two weeks ago. He was happy to see them growing well upright. Then they moved to the fish tank. The little colored fish were very beautiful and lively. Eleanor liked them heartily. They played with the fish by knocking at the outer wall of the glass tank. They were laughing, playing and talking. Then they moved to the back garden where the Dalmatian and the greyhound met them wagging their tails. Eleanor and Matt wiped their heads and their backs softly. Finally, they went to the teeter-totter and the swing yard. They both sat swinging joyfully.

XV

Suddenly, Jocelyn and another guy were exactly opposite to them. Eleanor saw her. She got down the swing and hurried to kiss and shake hands with Jocelyn. The latter felt unrest. Eleanor to Matt, "We haven't met since the university days." Then she turned to Jocelyn and said, "By the way, Jocelyn what did you do then? Did you return to the same university or you went to another one?" Jocelyn was quite disturbed and frightened. She gave an ironic smile and said, "You still remember! That was years ago. I had got my university degree long ago." She hedged. And then she turned to her companion and said, "Let's go, baby. Excuse me, Eleanor. See you."

Her answer was satisfying for Eleanor, but Matt took notice of it. It wasn't clear and direct to Eleanor's question. No further questions were asked. Neither Eleanor nor Matt could tell that man was one of the guests, one of Miese's factory laborers or not. Half an hour later, Matt apologized that he wanted to lie down on his bed. He parted Eleanor leaving her in the garden alone. She went back to the swing. As most of the guests went out of the house, Gillian felt hot and bored inside. With a glass of Champagne in her hand, she went for a walk in the front garden for fresh air. Then she turned aimlessly to the back garden. Factually, it was the fifth glass she had in an hour. She didn't trust her eyes or her ears when she glimpsed a couple in the dim light. They were between the shady trees in the back garden. That was Matt. She felt she got a bit tight after supper with those glasses of liquor and that cool silvery moonlight in the clear sky. Her heart was drumming and her eyes opened wide. Her abnormal vanity refused to believe what she had just seen, but she was quite unmistakable although their faces were partially obscured by the shadows. She went closer with unsteady steps to the place where the sound had come from. It was Matt and Jocelyn. Gillian buried her face in her hands and heavy tears filled from her eyes. There was silence for a moment or two. Then she called, "Matt! Matt! What're you doing there?" But none answered.

Gillian returned into the house to see Jocelyn coming out of Matt's room! "Is it possible? Matt's still too young for women like Jocelyn. What was she doing there? It's impossible! They were in the back garden a minute ago!" Gillian murmured to herself. She headed to Matt's room to find it ajar! She got into the room but Matt was sound asleep. She thought it was a trick. She put the light on. Amazing! Matt was really asleep. He rose up disturbed. "What's the matter, Mom?" She said nothing but turned back and left the room.

Gillian was at the edge of madness. She left the house and headed to the guests who gathered round the fireplace in the woods, just a few yards from the gate. Gillian thought she got tanked up on Champagne when she saw Jocelyn sitting on a chair at the gate. She had her hung nightgown and the night robe on. "Did she have the time to change so quickly?" Gillian murmured. And so she decided to get back into the house and wash her face with cold water. Then she poured a mug of coffee. She had a sip when she was consulting her mirror and fixing her make up.

As Gillian was in a gold lame evening gown and she was only five steps from the group round the fireplace, Fred Fetters acclimated and said aloud, "Oh, Princess of The Woods!" He moved a little to give her room to sit beside him. He was playing his clarinet. Another was singing. They were really happy that they were drinking, singing, talking and joking. The couples were enfolding one another.

Eleanor as well as the other guests heard explosions, bombing or shelling coming from the East; or from the boundary line between the two Afasinameas. Michael asked, "Is it the war again?" Fred Fetters; the engineer commented, "That's impossible. The two countries have democratic governments. And you know democracy and war don't match." But the explosions and the machine-gun shooting were more brutal and heavier. "There should be an exercise." Joseph said carelessly and asked, "Have any of you got a radio?" The chauffeur's wife had one on her mobile phone. They turned it on. There was nothing unusual in the West Afasinamea Broadcasting Service. When she turned it to East Afasinamea's, there was their national anthem played only. Fred nodded, but he said nothing. Michael looked at him disturbed and said, "There must be a coup in The East!" They were pole-avid by the news. Fred signed to him to hush.

Then Christina asked Michael to go into the house; she felt cold as she had only light clothes on and she wanted to get a rest before the dance party. In a few minutes all of them got into the house or into their tents as it was around ten pm and the dance party would start at ten-thirty. They all had to lie down for some rest and women had to dress for the dance party. Only Gillian and Fred remained.

Gillian felt happy to sit with a university-graduate engineer who could talk in politics, economics and technology and he was a professional clarinet player! Over and above, his round and large face was shone up and looked orange-red in the light of the burning fire with a permanent and natural sweet smile. Her mood improved and her smile returned to her face as she was sipping her coffee. She asked Mr. Fetters whether he would return to the fireplace after the dance party. He said he would. So, she gave instructions to the guard to take care of the fire and to keep it burning up to the next morning. When he rose up, she extended her hand to him to pull her up. She was unable to rise up by herself. Then she slipped her arm in his. She felt his warm body, and so she withdrew it and clung to his shoulder. Gillian had once read that it would be no harm if a woman encouraged a handsome man and that Fred was handsome; he was a very personable man, then she could take from him more than what she would take from her husband. Fred was educated, and of good personality. So, she found him the most suitable man to please him as he would please her. She was sure that he would please her more than Joe could do although the latter wasn't satisfied with her. He was busy with Jocelyn to satisfy each other.

At the dance time, Gillian addressed her guests saying, "We want you to spend a restful time in our country house. Make yourself comfortable! Please feel free!" Gillian knew how to keep her guests happy the time away at her reception. Then, with a jerk from her head, she indicated to the man on the PC and said enthusiastically aloud, "Music!" She laughed joyfully and she was nice to everyone. Then she withdrew aside to her husband and they started talking in a low voice. She seemed to be so laid-back.

As Jocelyn had no respect for any woman or any man, she came and slipped her hand in Joe's before she asked him softly and flirtingly, "You'll share me the first dance, Joe." She said and smiled charmingly. Gillian wondered whether that was an order or a request. Her face was puce with rage and her brows creased in a frown. Her cup ran over. She had hysterics but she was in a quandary. She wasn't that patient woman in such situations that she was a powder-keg going to explode right away. Jocelyn was going to pull him away but he resisted and drew back his arm, embarrassed. Not a word fell from his lips. With a side look at Gillian, he recognized how infuriated she was. Then he looked in her eyes with a light and shy smile imploringly. As she was always hot-headed in such an unexpected situation and abnormal behavior and to pacify her, Joseph winked at her giving an indication to calm down. Luckily, she could control herself and unbent. She looked in Jocelyn's eyes disdainfully. Words couldn't get out of her mouth and she wasn't going to spoil the party by asking her to leave. Suddenly, she had an idea. It was conciliation and so she acted at once. "Joe will share me the first dance and Mr. Dang will share you. The first dance is for the couples." Jocelyn looked over her shoulder at Gillian grudgingly and returned alone. Then Gillian looked in Joe's face and said, "I have never seen such appalling behavior. I don't know why you're very courteous with her. She needs a good talking to."

Matt and Eleanor sat at one table alone not far from the dancing couples. Matt had never danced before and none asked Eleanor to share him the dance. She was alone. Gillian and Joe danced together. So did Christina and Michael, Jocelyn and Robert and so on. After a few minutes, Jocelyn came to Gillian to allow her dance with Joe. Gill flushed disturbed, but she nodded and retired to Matt and Eleanor and joined them at their table. Then Jocelyn saw Eleanor and smiled at her. Eleanor answered the smile. As Gillian was observing them, she asked Eleanor whether she had known Jocelyn before. Eleanor said they were together in the university before Jocelyn was expelled, but they hadn't met since then. Matt and his mother together, "What? Expelled?" They were shocked. Eleanor's joy and the smile on her face died out. She hushed dead waiting for further explanation from Matt or from his mother. Then Matt smiled thoughtfully and said, "Miss Eleanor, do you remember when you asked her about the university an hour ago? She said she had got her university degree long ago." "Yes, I do. Why?" Eleanor said disturbed. "She hedged!" Matt added. Gillian smiled.

All the meanings of a smile waved on Gillian's face. She raised her head, opened her eyes and mind, but not her heart, and looked at nowhere below the ceiling. For an instant the discernible world disappeared gradually, and recollections and feelings appeared to be true. She was looking at Jocelyn in her memory teaching them, and skipping from one site to another. Three months passed, not three days or three weeks, and Jocelyn was unable to answer any question from the trial-exam samples, although the answers were always given at the bottom of the same page or on the following page. She remembered her flirting smiles and her winking at

Joe. She remembered all that had happened in the last three months. "We've been had!" She murmured.

Human beings are born with five senses. That was what science said and what they taught us at school. But Gillian, as well as a limited number of women, had additional five instincts. They were: the instinct of jealousy, curiosity, maternity, danger and the fifth one, the most important and the most dangerous, was the instinct of revenge. They were not exactly instincts because they were not temporal or casual; they looked like senses as they were born with them. Jocelyn had more. With denied remorse and lost dignity, the good and the evil were equal in her eyes.

Gillian saw Fred sitting at a table opposite to theirs. She gave him a sign to come and join them at their table. When she asked him why he was sitting and not dancing, he said he was single and alone. Then she introduced him to Eleanor, "Eleanor, this is Mr. Fetters. He's a mechanical engineer in our factory." Eleanor, "Nice to meet you, Mr. Fetters." Then Gillian turned to Fred Fetters and said, "Mr. Fetters, this is Eleanor; Matt's teacher. She's single and alone, too!" And she laughed. Mr. Fetters, "Nice to meet you, too, Eleanor." In a moment, Eleanor and Fred were dancing together. They were a great couple of dancers. Gillian was watching them. She murmured to herself, "Educated people are educated in everything!" Eleanor and Fred looked very happy. They fell for each other instantly that they spent the time talking, smiling and of course dancing. Hadn't Gillian herself introduced them to each other, she'd think they had acquainted with each other long ago.

XVI

At the very beginning, when Jocelyn had sex with Joseph and got from him much more than she did from any other man she had slept with before, she knew that sex in the Mieses' married life then wasn't so good; its heat was toning down and it should be suffering from lack of energy. As they were of unpolished culture, they would never think to work together to regain the excitement of love. When she asked him whether he had ever sent his wife a romantic message on her cell phone, he roared with laughter and said she had never been far from him. Jocelyn then curved her eye brows and gave an ironic smile. She fancied their marriage broken sooner or later as Joseph was looking for satisfaction from her. She was younger than Gillian and more experienced in love affair and so she was able to split that marriage and get Joseph. She decided to steal him from his wife!

After the dance party, all were tired. Nevertheless, Jocelyn withdrew outside the house for fresh air. In the night, the guests in tents could enjoy the soft cold breeze, the crickets' chirping, the owls' hoot and the wolves' howling which were disturbing and terrifying to some of them, but they were natural and interesting music to others. She sat on a rocking chair by the pond and placed her feet on its rim. She saw Gillian getting into Matt's room a few minutes ago and so she expected Joe any time to walk out. She had to move quickly. Therefore, she hasted to her room and dressed for the third time that night. She chose a new pink tulle gown which she didn't bring with her and which was of course so light and lace that she looked naked. So, she had better put her yellow robe on her shoulders and then she turned back to the same chair. Her robe was open to show some little black thing which could hardly be called V-thong, without a bra and that her gown could be seen with difficulty. She extended her legs, leaned her head on the back of the chair and closed her eyes. Only a few minutes later, she heard heavy tread of someone on the front-garden drive. When she opened her eyes and looked, Joe was going out for a walk along a track on the side of the river. He always felt a strong desire to have a one-mile walk after and before meals and when he felt bored. Gillian always encouraged him to walk before and after meals to sharpen his appetite or for digestion. In addition to that, he could sleep well in the night and he would eat a lot and store more energy.

It seemed that Joseph didn't notice Jocelyn as there was a big tree between them. She rose up holding her robe and called, "Hey Joe! Why are you so speedy?" She laughed charmingly, hasted and slipped her arm into his when he was two yards out of the gate on his way to the south; towards the river. Joe didn't say any word. "I thought you might need some company." Joe kept silent. Then she added, "Do you mind if I join you?" "No, I'd be happier to have your company." He answered. "I felt bored alone. I'll be an amusing companion. Trust me!" She asserted. Joe slowed as she clung to his arm. Then Joe said, "What you did in the dancing hall was mean and underhand."

Jocelyn was surprised. In a moment, she said apologizing, "Perhaps, unintentionally, I did something offended her. But I didn't mean it." Although he remained unconvinced, he was thrilled when he felt her scent, her light gown and her warm and soft flesh.

The giant oak-tree tops on either side of the track at the bank of the river met forming a series of domes overhead, putting the place into darkness. Only indirect and faint starlight could reach them. Jocelyn turned from the track to a clump of giant oaks in the forest to the left, not far from the edge, claiming that she felt tired and wanted to get some rest. When they sat under a large tree, she jumped and sat in his lap, "It's so harsh to my soft skin and I'm scared of scorpions!" They were safe from ramblers' eyes. Actually, Jocelyn wasn't scared of anything, nor was she tired. She was burning. That was on one hand and on the other she had the intent to revenge Gillian by stealing her husband.

Robert Dang was under the same tree behind its trunk, next to Joe and Jocelyn. She was exactly lying on his chest, leaning her head down on his face and kissing him. They had nothing on; they were as naked as little babies had just come to life. "I have been watching you for quite a little time; since you left the track and turned to the trees." He said when he was drawing nearer to them. Joseph smiled thoughtfully. He was warned by something inside him. It seemed that the time for hatred, disgust and repent had come. "It was a plan of Jocelyn. In a minute, this guy will black-mail me. He's no more than henpecked." He murmured. "What are you doing here?" Jocelyn asked Robert amazed. "It's emergent . . . ." He said. She interrupted him and turned to

Joseph and said, "Joe, give him fifty dollars and let him go away! He can't control his tongue!" Jocelyn suggested. Both were generous; Jocelyn with her body and Joe had to be with his money. Joseph had no option. The May-Day celebrity in the country house would turn to be scandal if he didn't.

Meantime, Gillian closed Matt's room door and walked to the fireplace where Fred Fetters was sitting alone playing a melancholic tune on his clarinet. Gillian joined him and sat next to him listening attentively. She was touched with the tune. They were alone. When he was playing on his clarinet, Gill was playing with his hair. The tune was wonderful and she liked it very much. When Fred paused to have his breath again, she supported her head on his shoulder. He patted her hair and pressed her shoulder with the other hand. They both felt the new warmth, adjusted their position to have Gill on his lap; between his arms and hers wrapped his neck. When she had the lace of her robe loose, the whole place smelled with lavender. She stood up and extended her hand to Fred to stand up.

Gillian had known each tree, bush and shrub in the forest close to their country house. She led him to a close clump of oak trees opposite to the house. When they started moving to the depth of the forest, Gill slipped her arm through his and said, "I was waiting for you to rise up. I didn't know you would waste the night playing your clarinet only!" She leaned on his shoulder, his arm wrapped her waist and they went deeper in the woods. After five trees and under an assigned one, Gillian preceded him one step forward, turned and wrapped his neck with her arms. He was waiting for that moment. He hugged her and they both kissed. She undid his shirt buttons. Then the two couples;

Joe and Jocelyn in the south and Fred and Gillian in the north were spending a nice time simultaneously in two parallel, and equal lines, similar to the least triviality.

After half an hour, the two couples met at the gate. They got into the front garden together and sat around the round pond. One of the servers brought them cold cans of beer. Fred apologized and said he didn't drink alcohol. The servant could provide him with a glass of lemonade, any fruit juice or some other fizzy drink. After another half an hour, Gillian was very tired and she was yawning. She rose up, paid them good night and went into her bedroom. Fred resumed playing his clarinet. Joe and Jocelyn liked the tune very much that they sat with Fred until a late hour in the night.

Gillian couldn't sleep as she was alone in the bedroom. Her husband had to be sociable to his guests. When he joined her at a late hour, he was pleased to see her sound asleep. He smiled and yawned, undressed quickly and went to bed. She, too, was pleased that he didn't try to awaken her although she was awake thinking of Fred Fetters. Her mood ranged between repentance and joy, anger and pleasure, sadness and happiness and between desire and neglect. Then she had to console herself and to put an end for all of that self-suffering, she murmured, "Nothing and none is complete."

Both of Gill and Joe were satisfied sexually. She loved Joe and she was happy with him. He was the only man in her life. Joe was as the same as Gillian. He was happy with her. He loved her and he would love her forever. Both were straight and satisfied. Those educated people spoiled the Mieses' life. It would sound better to say that the surplus energy, wealth, boredom, long free time, inferiority of lack of education and finally isolation all pushed both of them far to be a prey for any crook who was sexually or financially hungry.

XVII

After breakfast on the second of May, the engineer in Meese's factory Mr Fred Fetters asked the guests who had gathered under a large shady tree in the forest opposite to Mr Meese's house, about love, money, peace and happiness and whether they were referring to one thing. Many of them spoke about love, a few spoke shyly about sex, more spoke about money but none spoke about peace or happiness. They almost said that one couldn't live without sex and love; to be in love or to be loved. One of them said he wanted both; to love and to be loved. Shouts of hails roared. Another said that he wanted a single, beautiful and young woman to love. Christina corrected his view point saying he had better see an ophthalmologist as soon as possible. They acclimated and burst with laughter. Another one, a gay, said he wanted a unique relation with a handsome man. Women dropped their heads and smiled shyly. A woman said that women, and she was one of them, preferred to be loved before they loved. The first step should be taken by the man. Matt acclimated joyfully. So did Eleanor. Jocelyn crossed and turned her face away. Gillian shook her head opposing. None talked about happiness or peace or they were hardly defined, and without a shape.

Complementary questions followed about the elements of happiness, together with their answers: love and making love, a lot of money, good friends and good health. When they were asked to add any more elements, they looked thoughtful, hesitative, and shaky and they felt unable. A few of them added secondary elements, as education or a degree, a child or children, travel, arts, sports, spending a holiday in the country or at the sea shore or just labour.

Matt added a central question, "Can people enjoy any of these points aside from safety, security and peace which are the natural products of the civil rights, freedoms and democracy?" Michael, Fred, Christina and all the guests stopped talking. Matt's words were unexpected and they were to the point. His father, Mr Joseph Miese, stood up, crossed his arms on his flattened chest, gave a smile of satisfaction, raised his head high up and nodded strongly. He was completely satisfied. The engineer, Mr Fetters, was the first to talk after that stunning pause, "Ok Matt. In a democratic environment, who's happier; one with money and love but diseased, or one with money and healthy but without love or one healthy with a warm love but penniless." Faces turned left and right looking at each other. One of them commented in a low voice, "Because he's an engineer and educated with a degree, he has ideas almost about everything." Mr Joseph Miese raised his eye brows and murmured, "Oh, what a wonderful man you are, Mr Fetters! Culture, a degree and science have priority to speak aloud!" He looked at him jealous. He made a sigh of sorrow and turned back to his house. On his way he wished his country house had been full of guests, with a lot of beautiful girls with degrees.

Meantime, Gillian was approaching and she was very pleased to hear Matt talking to the engineer and to the others, conversing about happiness, democracy, love, peace, universities and engineering branches. Mr. Fetters was a mechanic engineer. Her son preferred civil engineering. They were talking and laughing. She went straight to them. Her sweet scent advanced her and filled the place. She was interested to go to the beauty salon before the guests came. Then she was careful to keep her make up last fresh by gazing at herself in the mirror and fixing it so many times in the last few hours. She was a real star. All praised her beauty. Mr. Fetters received her hailing, "Oh, look! Who's coming! Miss Star! Your dress is absolutely adorable. Wow!" They laughed pleasantly. She started, "How delightfully warm the morning is!" They exchanged a few words, Gillian sat between Mr. Fetters and Matt listening, watching and laughing. Then Matt had their permission and went to his room to relax before he could return to his books. Most of them rose and dispersed. Gillian took notice of Jocelyn's looks and winks at Joe who was standing at the gate preoccupied of something. Then they both headed to the southern side of the forest together. Gillian gestured with her hand hinting to Fred to go for a walk. An eye for an eye! She slipped her arm into his and started slowly to the thick clump of trees in the woods which they both had known well last night. She was listening most of the time. When she spoke, she only asked a short question or answered it in her distinctive 'Yeah!' The more words she heard from Mr. Fetters, the more wonderful she felt him. He was talking in some other way; soft, so attractive and more touching than Joe's. By his sweet chosen words, he sent her to the edge of thrill madness. He pictured life in a striking curios way. Her face was rosy with amusement when she was listening to him. When they came to a darker place; completely shady, she freed her arm from his and wrapped his neck, leaning her head on his chest. He extended his free hand and wrapped her waist. Then they both pressed tight. They moved only three yards when he turned to her, wrapped her waist with his arms and kissed. He was so thirsty to get a little of her nectar which he tasted last night. She kissed Joe and Joe kissed her thousands and thousands times, but Fred's kissing was different. Fred's day—kissing was much more thrilling than his night one. Last night she got much from Fred but it seemed she was going to take much more on that day. When he was moving his lips and tongue checking her neck and her lips so smoothly, so slowly and mutely, she lost control on her hands and on her organs. She was trembling subconscious. She felt his hot breath on her neck. She started moaning, pulling and pressing his head to her breast. She was drooping and finally she was worn out. He carried her on his arms to another tree she pointed at. It was quite shady and dark; thicker and darker than the first one. He made her lie on a sandy place and lay on her kissing every square inch of her excited body as he tenderly made her strip off her clothing. After a few minutes, they were sweating, panting and lying side by side, weary and silent. It was the second time with the second man in her life. The first was Joseph. "Oh, how wonderful Fred is! They don't study this stuff at the university, do they?" She wondered breathlessly, unable to speak. She gasped and closed her eyes with the utmost of joy. She got the ultimate thrill.

Joseph Miese rang the guard in the country house two days ago. He told him to hire two workers, two servers and two Paris-trained chefs who can cook special romantic meals, grill fish, chicken, red meat indoor and outdoor and more. The two workers had to build a fireplace on a patch in the woods they both had known well. He told him also that they had to dig a hole close to the fireplace exactly in the barrel size and depth. There should be not less than twenty-five pieces of dry logs piled up beside that fireplace. Since the guard was unable to understand, Joseph scorned him harshly and said. "You needn't understand. Just do what I tell you!"

When they got to the place on Sunday morning, Joseph and Michael set a barrel in the hole. The barrel looked like a large pipe with its open bottom. Its rim was at the ground-surface level. Therefore, the hole should be deepened another two inches. At eleven-thirty, the guard lit a fire in the barrel and another one in the fireplace. The barrel was almost red hot at twelve-thirty and the fireplace was ablaze. A metal net with half-inch meshes was set directly over the blazing logs in the barrel. Four cooking casseroles were prepared. The first large one was almost full of water, large pieces of red meat, veggies, salt and spices. The second one, also large, was full of pieces of well spiced fowl, stag and hare meat. Then the third casserole, which was smaller than the first two, as well as the fourth, was full of onion, vegetables, chili and tomatoes with a glassful of olive oil and the fourth, which was set beside it, was half-full of damp rice and a little salt only. On the contrary of the first two casseroles which were firmly closed, the last two were left open. Another two nets, similar to the first one in the bottom, stuffed with salted walnut-size pieces of meat between, were set over the two open casseroles. The barrel was closed firmly and thickly covered with pebbles and soil.

The two workers set a large table on an even surface under the nearest carob tree with dozens of different large trays, bowls, dishes, glasses, spoons, forks, knives, tissues, a large tray full of green salad, lemons and boxes of soft, cold fizzy drinks and beer cans on. Well-spiced and flavored pork and venison was to be roasted on the left side of the fireplace. Fowl of all kinds and fish were to be roasted on the right side. When they were well roasted, they removed the soil and opened the barrel. Clouds of vapor climbed high up in the air out of the barrel. The whole place up to hundreds of feet away was filled with the smell of roasted, fried, cooked and well-spiced meat. Foxes, stray dogs, wild cats, jackals, field mice and rats were so curious that they drew nearer to the barbecue place slowly and cautiously. Hyenas and wolves were watching at a further distance. The guests, who previously said they wouldn't feel hungry until sunset, had their appetite sharpened by the irresistible smell of the well-cooked, fried and roasted meat, poultry and seafood. The women, who were interested in diets and regime, as well as some men, ate shyly and slowly at the beginning. Since their appetite was sharpened, they felt starved. "This food is exquisite," One of the women said. She helped herself to a second plate. Generally, they emptied their plates once and twice. Some of them had to refill theirs for the third time. But a few of them, only a few, filled their dishes for the fourth time! "The food is fabulous." One of the women on regime said. They came at the food greedily and they got full. To avoid constipation, each of them had a lot of salad, more than one can of beer or soft drink in addition to glasses of cold water. They got full, unable to eat or drink any more things. Nevertheless, when the plates were shining as if they were wiped out, they licked their lips where some salty fat was. Then they shambled to the nearest cedar and oak trees and lay down. They wondered where that food was common. Michael told them he had known about it in the Internet. It was common in the Mediterranean countries and in the Sahara-Desert states in Africa. Together with the Dangs, the guard, the two hired workers, the chauffeur and his wife, and those who could lend a hand, the Mieses had to clean the place, the utensils and to put things in place. The house was a bee-hive like. They all worked hard; cleaning, wiping out and replacing utensils in the kitchen, sweeping, brushing and checking everything.

XVIII

After lunch and at three-thirty, it was time for the surprise which the Mieses had prepared. It was a voyage by boat in the river. In addition to their own one, Joe hired another two boats. Only couples should compete first, and then the bachelors in pairs. The winners would get a valuable prize. Once they found a mark, only one mark, on any of the small islets in the river, they had to bring it back to the shore. It was a manmade object.

Michael and Christina got onboard the first one. He helped her get into the twelve-foot long boat that was rocking and swaying as she stepped on. She sat in a light-metal seat and Michael took the back seat and started the engine. They headed out of the queue to an islet they had chosen. It was next to the opposite side of the river; less than one mile from the start point; close to the boundary line between the two Afasinameas. Probably, it was the smallest islet they had ever seen but they were fascinated by its prickly shrubs with two or three large berries. When they beached the boat and jumped out onto the shore, it wasn't more than the Mieses' estate in surface. Nevertheless, they had to look well before they stepped on although it was impossible to move even one foot forward on that islet. They returned to the boat and sailed round it. Finally, they decided to go to another one as it was impossible to go through all those prickly shrubs.

Then Michael had an idea. Christina would ride on his shoulders to look down on the islet, hoping she could see anything that looked like a manmade object. It was fun. Christina was very pleased to sit on Michael's shoulders. Luckily, she glimpsed a sack of three books at the end of a reptile track. Michael would go crawling on his hands, chest and abdomen to get them. When he tried to put her down, she clung to his neck amiably. She was fascinated by the breathtaking view of the river with its blue clear water, its dark green islets and with the comfortable sit on Michael's shoulders. She stuck on his shoulders holding his head with her two hands. As they wasted time, he warned her either she got down or he would sling her into the water. And so, she jumped down quickly. Michael crawled as fast as he could. He got the books and they returned fast to the queue where the others were waiting for them. The books were wrapped with a blue ribbon and they had no time to untie it and open the books. They were laughing, hugging each other, and dreaming of the prize. When Joe saw the books still wrapped, he recognized they hadn't opened any of them. Regardless of the time they wasted, their boat was the first. There were two wedding rings in an envelope in one of the books. Those two gold rings were their prize. Gillian commented, "Well, you've got the wedding rings, but when is the wedding day?" Christina looked at Michael shyly, but he dropped his head dreaming and unknowing what to say. They preceded the second boat by ten minutes although the three boats started almost at the same time.

Fred and Eleanor got onboard the second boat. There were two islets close to each other. They chose the first right one which wasn't so far from the river bank. The two islets looked twins, but the one on the right was a little larger than the first one on the left. Eleanor complained that it was impossible to find a track to follow among all those blackthorns, hawthorns, prickly pears, and berries in addition to many little shrubs and bushes which were all thorny. Therefore, they moved to the other islet on the left which was less than a hundred yards away. It looked white or it was rather beige. When they arrived it, they found it abounded with wild flowers; daffodils, tulips, and blossoming bushes. The whole islet was hedged with white-rose jasmine bushes. "We're lucky, Eleanor!" Fred said aloud pleasantly. They beached the boat and then Fred jumped onto the islet and tied the rope to a jasmine stem. He held Eleanor's waist and carried her from the boat. She hung to his neck and lifted her feet up. She liked Fred holding her waist which hadn't been held for more than a year. When they stepped forward onto the islet, Eleanor climbed up a small rock which was a chair-height and looked at the breathtaking roses and flowers that covered the whole islet. "Amazing! Look! It's a beautiful garden of daffodils, tulips and jasmines. It's astonishing; the most wonderful and real beauty one can imagine." She shouted with joy. Eleanor was right. One more beautiful thing she forgot; it was the islet dwellers. They were birds only. As the whole roses and flowers on the islet were seedless and fruitless, birds didn't damage the plants in search for food. The islet was about two thousand square yards. Not a prickly bush was growing there. It seemed as if someone had plucked up all the other weeds and wild shrubs. The whole islet was filled with the aroma of daffodils and jasmines. They searched each square inch but there wasn't any manmade object on that islet. Eleanor suggested they could pluck a bouquet of roses and flowers each and get back. Fred nodded and started with the daffodils. So did Eleanor. They returned to their boat and turned back to the start quay. Both were polite in their words, conducts and their clothes were respectful, too. Nevertheless, they looked very happy and they were laughing. They understood each other.

Joe and Gillian burst with laughter when they saw the two big bouquets of flowers. Then Joe said, "Unless you're educated, you won't return with these bouquets of roses and flowers only. They're the manmade object! You'll get five dollars for each rose or flower! You didn't search for the manmade object long, did you?" Eleanor and Fred looked at each other and burst with laugher.

They looked around for Mr. Dang but he wasn't there. Jocelyn said he had a bad headache and he was asleep. As Jocelyn disliked missing such a voyage, a single worker volunteered to be her companion. They were happy and smiling when they set off their voyage. But when they returned half an hour later than the second boat, Jocelyn and her companion, Mr. Rampler, were disappointed with dark faces. They were empty-handed. Neither Jocelyn said anything about the voyage, nor did anyone ask her. Then Joseph asked Mr. Rampler whether they could find any object on the islet which they went to. Rampler drew a long breath and turned his face away for a moment. Then he looked at Jocelyn disdainfully and said, "When we beached the boat and I stepped onto that islet, the lady saw a rattle snake. She shouted and groaned and stuck to the boat. That damned snake was rising its head up and gazing at us defiantly. I had no choice but to return to the boat. When I screwed my head and looked back, it was still in its place. I suggested going to another islet and the lady nodded. When she heard the water splashing next to the second islet, she was scared of alligators. She made her mind to return. As the water was shallow by the islet, we moved at a snail pace and so we were late." Joseph and Gillian roared with laughter that their tears fell down on their cheeks. Finally Joseph could control himself for a moment and said, "That was the manmade object! The rattle snake is a dummy. It's made of plastic and there's a gold bracelet inside it!" All the attendants burst with laughter. It was a surprise! Jocelyn couldn't control herself any more. She was so angry that she dashed to Joe shouting with intent to scratch his face, but Fred grabbed her arm and told her firmly to get back. None of the other guests was desirous to go for a boat ride after that incident.

The guard noticed that the door which led to the flat roof was unlocked. He told Mr. Miese who in turn told him carelessly to lock it. The house returned to its previous five-star condition. A little before sunset, they all got out of the gate and straight into their cars. The Mieses stood at the gate waving their hands and giving the guests a 'Bye-bye'. Just before getting into the car, Gillian remembered her sable coat. She was turning back when Joseph said it was warm and it would be all the same if she left it there until the next fall. But she went straight to her closet to find it missing. She called the guard aloud. Joseph heard her. Together with the guard, they both climbed upstairs to the bedroom. The three Mieses, the Dangs, the chauffeur and his wife, the two servers and the guard all raked around for Gillian's expensive coat everywhere in the house. They searched far and wide for it that they turned the recliners and the chairs upside down, one by one, looked under the seats and under the beds, searched in the dresser, in the closets, under the tables in and under the trees in the front and back gardens. Even the bathrooms and the toilets were searched. Then Joe told the guard to unlock the roof door and to look on the roof. Gillian said, "But that door was locked more than a year ago and it was still locked." Joe was surprised and doubt filled his mind. "It was unlocked an hour ago and I myself told the guard to lock it." Joseph said and turned to the guard and asked him, "Are you sure the roof door was unlocked and you looked it?" The guard nodded. Gillian herself hasted to that door, unlocked and opened it by herself. She was stunned to find recent footsteps of a man on the fallen leaves and on the damp dust on the roof. She shouted aloud, "Someone had climbed up to the roof." They all climbed up across that door to examine what she had seen. They took pictures of the footsteps by their cellular phones with intent to report to the police. None was suspected. They shook hands with all the guests and gave them a farewell at the outer gate. None of them was holding anything that looked like the missing sable coat. "I can't believe it! Our visitors never do such dreadful things; impossible!" Gillian said shocked. Joseph said, "Let's check all of the expensive devices."

He went to the bedroom and Gillian went to the kitchen. The vase in the kitchen was missing. "Joe, the vase! It's missing!" Gillian wailed in agony. "And the clock, Gill! It's missing, too!" Joe said aloud.

The nearest police station was in Lateburg. They turned to their cars and drove to Lateburg. At the southern outskirt of the town, there was a car accident. A truck collided with a taxi crushing it. The inquiry absolved the truck driver of all responsibility of the accident. The taxi driver was drunk. Traffic stopped. There was a man lying dead on the street. It was the taxi driver; Jocelyn's man. Another man was also killed. He was still in the car. An officer; a Major, stepped forward and uncovered the face of the first man on the street. He stood stunned. Then he asked another officer whether there were any other casualties in the accident, the officer pointed at the car. When the Major looked inside the crashed car, he stood still unable to say any word. He remembered his previous colleague Bruce Sompler who was killed more than eight years ago. The two men were the killers. He shook his head and then he nodded. Finally, he looked up at the sky and said, "How just Heaven is!"

To the Mieses' amazement, Jocelyn was in a state of shock, sobbing and incoherent. Abruptly she screamed, wailed and cried in agony. Was she losing another big opportunity again, perhaps the last? The dead man's face was covered with a sable coat, blood-spotted and oily. It was Gillian's missing coat! The ambulance came and took the two dead men. "Why are you crying? Are they blood relatives of yours?" Gillian asked her with an incredulous look. Jocelyn came to herself. What an uncharacteristic mistake she did! "No, no, they aren't. But the sight of blood and the dead scares me." Jocelyn said. In fact, Jocelyn was crying because she was misused by the man whom she thought he loved her, but she found out she was under illusion. He was a murderer! Jocelyn might commit mistakes, but she had never thought of stealing anything valuable or worthless; she felt betrayed. "Damn it! He not only took the coat, but he broke his promise to leave that damned stuff in Gillian's closet." Jocelyn murmured.

It was the first time in his life, Joseph felt sorry for someone without feeling contemptuous. It was the first time he ever approached understanding any other human feelings.

XIX

On the contrary of Jocelyn, Mrs. Miese respected, trusted and highly estimated Eleanor. So did Mr. Miese with a little extra thing; he lusted after her. As Jocelyn left the place suddenly; early in the morning of the second day, they needed a tutor to replace her. Gillian said that Eleanor had started a privet school of her own. She was a teacher and a graduate and so they could hire her. Joseph nodded and he didn't oppose her. Gillian looked for Eleanor's cellular number and called her. Both knew that Eleanor hadn't enough time to go to Hungupville late in the afternoon or in the morning and to turn back to Lateburg on the same day. She was interested in her school. In her free time, she had to care for her daughter but there should be a way to help them. Therefore, Gillian called to tell her they were paying her a visit next Saturday afternoon.

When they got into her small flat in Lateburg, Eleanor had only her nightgown on. She asked their permission to dress, but Gillian said that she was ok and she didn't need to dress. They felt at home. Then Eleanor put the headphones on her ears, talking to them and to the picture of somebody on the webcam, typing, sending and receiving instant messages all at the same time. Curious and amazed, Gillian couldn't control herself and be patient.

She wondered what Eleanor was doing. The latter raised her head to catch Joseph gazing at her bare leg. She looked at him sharply and scornfully. It was the daring way his eyes looked with an unacceptable manner of impertinence. He was gazing at Eleanor's bare leg as if he had owned her. She put the headphones aside, signed to Gillian to wait and went straight into the bathroom to dress. She turned back to her lap top, replacing the headphones on her ears. She told them she had started chatting with someone only a few minutes before they came in. That encouraged them to tell her about their online study. When Gillian looked at Joe, he jerked his head and winked at her to talk to Eleanor. Therefore Gillian started, "Eleanor, we'll get right into the point. We've a problem we can't solve. We need your help."

When Eleanor heard their story, she encouraged them and offered to help them as far as she could. Joe and Gillian exchanged glanced with a faint smile of joy on their faces and implored her to do her best to help them. She went to the site of that online university and got an idea about the curriculum. She said she was unable to go to Hungupville for lack of free time in the work days. She could help them by emails and by other electronic communication channels, but she can meet them in the weekends.

She promised to send both of them full lessons, explained, simplified and summarized in the following twenty-four hours. Then she showed them how to sign up an email and chatting accounts. Gillian looked at Joseph and said teasing him, "Ladies first!" They liked the idea. It wasn't only easy, but it was useful and amusing. They could befriend with people all over the world. They could call and ask her if they face any problem concerning their study.

They also had the chance to contact her by email and by chatting. Gillian typed Eleanor's email ID and saved it in her cellular phone as a draft message.

The Mieses invited Eleanor to spend the next weekend and every weekend with them in Hungupville. She could spend the night with her daughter in one of the bedrooms inside their villa or in the garden rooms where the Dangs lived. Eleanor accepted and preferred the garden rooms. Then they promised to pay her as a part timer. She hushed and flushed and felt so shy that she dropped her eyes down to the floor for a long instant. Then she raised her head up. Her face was still red with a broad smile on. She said she didn't hint at getting a job behind her offer to help them and she added that they needed not hesitate to ring her anytime; day or night. Then at the door of Eleanor's room when they were getting out, Gillian opened her handbag and handed Eleanor a small parcel. Eleanor unwrapped it instantly to have the lavender-air filling the room. Joseph was surprised. It was one of the vessels he bought last week on their wedding anniversary. Eleanor was very pleased that she kissed Gillian on her two cheeks. Joseph wished she had raised her head to kiss him, too! When they got into the car and they were waving to her, Eleanor said aloud, "If you need anything anytime, just gimme a ring."

On their way to their house, Gillian asked Joseph suddenly whether he had got any word from Jocelyn. He was surprised. With a faint smile in his eyes he said she hadn't called or written to him, nor she said she would.

The time they returned home, Gillian hurried to the study, turned the PC on and sat in the seat. Joe followed her tiptoeing. He held her between his arms and carried her to the recliner, far from the PC in the study. Then he hasted back to the PC, sat in the seat opposite to it and looked over his shoulder at Gillian. When he saw her agitated and oppressed, he promised to buy her a new lap top, similar to Eleanor's, but of the latest model. He would do that on the next day before getting back home. She wiped the tears on her cheeks, and walked to Joe. She wrapped his neck with her arms watching him signing in to chat, then to his new email. Finally, he signed out and said, "It's your turn, Gill." Gillian did the same and then she turned the PC off. He rose up and carried Gillian who was wrapping his neck with her arms and went straight into the bedroom. Matt saw them. He said teasing them, "Congratulation! Just married!" Gillian burst with laughter, enjoyed but Joseph smiled delightfully and pressed her to his chest tenderly and passionately.

On the second day, Gillian opened the door of the back-garden rooms to find them abounding with lice, fleas and flies. The floor was littered with fag ends. She called Joseph to look in the rooms. When he saw that mess, he demeaned himself. "How could that educated, beautiful and well-dressed woman be in that dirt? It is unbelievable! She isn't a human being!" Then he remembered Christina's words about Jocelyn, "She is a devil!" And he murmured, "What a stupid bastard I was!" and kicked the table that the empty glasses and dirty bowls jumped down to the floor. His passion for her made him blind of everything in the past weeks. Gill was observing him and smiling. Then she said, "She thought she could fool us, but I got wise to her." In reality, it was Robert's responsibility to clean the place and to take care of it. Jocelyn always scorned him.

They started the lessons and they were advancing many folds of what they had done with Jocelyn. Eleanor introduced the lessons in a way much better than Jocelyn's. It was easy, simple and comprehensible. It was acceptable by heart and mind. When Eleanor sent them the first lesson, at about seven pm upon their request, she had prepared it to match with their needs and capabilities. The subject of that lesson was the 'Schools of Literature'.

In fact, it covered more than one subject; literarily and historically. She started with the oldest writing: Classicism. The language was complicated far from symbolism, similes, and metaphors. Beauty of nature, modern prose and musical words or expressions had not been used then. She said in her emailed lesson that all the old writing before the eighteenth century AD was mostly classical. Greek, early English, European and Asian writers and writings were all classical. She added names of some old writers, known all over the world, including John Milton, William Shakespeare and Sophocles. She quoted a little from their original writing which was translated or rewritten in modern English and explained, simplified and summarized the quoted paragraphs to be comprehensible to the Mieses. She told them as there were Gods and Goddesses in the Greek literary works, without the least reference to Christianity, The Lord or The Bible, it meant that Christianity had not been known yet. In other words, old Greek literature was known more than two thousand years ago. All kinds of literature all over the world were written in verse. Prose, what we read in books and in newspapers, what we hear in movies currently, wasn't known then. Joseph and Gillian understood well every word Eleanor had written and sent. They were not less than two hardworking students and they were very pleased to be students again. On comparing Eleanor's lessons to Jocelyn's, Gillian didn't find any relationship between Jocelyn and teaching. Joseph smiled thoughtfully but maliciously. On comparing between them, he found a big similarity between the two women as women, not taking teaching into consideration.

An hour later, they received another email from Eleanor. It was a checking-understanding exercise. She told them they would see five paragraphs below quoted from books written in different ages and belonged to different schools of literature. They had to decide which were classic and which were not. They did reply the email in a few minutes and sent it to Eleanor. Only an instant later, Gillian's phone rang. It was Eleanor. She congratulated them on their correct answers. They were very happy. After a word of praise from the two sides, they thanked her and hung up. The want for a degree and for a social position made Joseph study the whole subject and memorize it. He was more serious and more enthusiastic than Gillian although she was a hardworking student, too.

Joseph was looking at Gillian amazed with a faint smile on his face. She looked busy-minded. She was thinking of what a mistake she had committed when she asked Joseph to change her choice from English to History. She blamed herself bitterly but she was shy to ask him to change her choice again from History to English. He would lose his temper and she would be the contempt of his sharp tongue which he could rarely control. Then the idea flashed in her brain. She would do that by herself, but Joseph would see her and he would laugh long. He would pat on his chest, flatter it and repeat his easy-difficult saying. Finally, she decided to do that by herself, rainy or clear! She turned to the PC, held the mouse and pointed at that university site. Joseph was watching her, "You aren't going to take your first exam, are you?" He said teasing her. As his tone was amiable and soft, she told him what she was going to do. Suddenly he frowned. She was worried and terrified when he smacked his forehead. Then he smiled (She felt a little peace) and said, "I forgot! Your choice is still English." She sprang up joyfully, hugged and gave him a long, warm and passionate kiss.

Next Saturday, Joe went home earlier than usual. He had stomachache with fever. Only an hour later Fred Fetters rang him saying there was a big problem in the factory. The temperature in the boiler rose excessively and the cooling system wasn't working properly. Consequently the main conveying belt had broken and a part of the engine components melted. A few minutes later, it was burning and the smoke was choking in the place. Unfortunately, there was complete breakdown. The whole production section needed maintenance and some spare parts. He took pictures of the bad parts and wrote their reference numbers in his notebook. The general manager couldn't do anything as Joseph hadn't given him authority concerning maintenance. Since Joseph Miese, the factory president and owner, was ill unable to go to the factory, he asked the engineer to come to his house to see what they would do.

Meanwhile, Eleanor and her child Mattie arrived at the Mieses'. Gillian led them to the study. Joe, from the bedroom, phoned his wife and told her that Mr. Fetters, the engineer, was coming. A little more than half an hour, Fred Fetters was ringing the doorbell and Gillian herself answered the door. Fred was surprised to find himself face to face with her alone. His eyes shone up and a broad smile was drawn on his face. He opened his arms to wrap her waist and bent to kiss her but she gave him a swift turn-of-the-cheek move. He was embarrassed and his arms drooped slowly to his sides. His eyes lost their shining and the smile fainted on his face. She led him to the study where Eleanor and her child were sitting. "Hello, Eleanor! What're you doing here?" Fred Fetters started smiling. Eleanor stood up and shook hands with him. "Be seated Mr. Fetters. Joe's coming in a minute." Gillian said. He sat in a seat opposite to Eleanor. Gillian left for the bedroom to tell Joe that Mr. Fetters had come. Fred was embarrassed, frustrated, and disappointed, but he turned to be quite happy when he saw Eleanor who soon looked to be preoccupied. She was thinking of her daughter, of the joys of the past, of the future expectations with their perhaps, maybes, possibilities and impossibilities. She was thinking of the Mieses; their simplicity, fortune, ignorance, happiness, peace and ambitions. She was thinking of Gillian, of her kind heart, of her good intentions and of her unawareness.

Fred started, "What's your name, kitten?" He asked the six-year-old child. Eleanor smiled and turned her face to her kid encouraging her to answer. The kid smiled shyly and while looking at her mother she said, "Mattie." "Oh, what a sweet name! Gimme a kiss on my cheek, Mattie." Her mother winked at her encouraging and so Mattie went quickly to Fred and kissed him on his cheek. "Oh, a smart kitten!" He said holding her between his arms. He asked her how old she was. Eleanor said she was only six. Then Fred asked her teasingly why she was late for school on that day.

Her eyes shone with joy and her face was lit with a big smile before she gave a negative answer with her index finger and said, "Mom's my teacher." "Oh! Really?" He commented aiming at Eleanor with his question. Eleanor nodded. Then again to Mattie, "And your dad, what's he?"

The child whitened unexpectedly. She dropped down her head and a tear fell from her large hazel eyes. She left Fred and went back broken-hearted to her Mom who held her against her breast, patted on her back and wiped her smooth hair. Eleanor herself was resisting a painful tear not to fall down from her eye. Fred was stunned. His face darkened. Then he asked, "What's the matter, Madam? I don't understand anything. Did I commit a mistake?" Eleanor wiped her face with both her hands giving her fingers a chance to wipe those shy tears in her eyes. She raised her head and said, "Her father Cecil Pearce . . ." Fred interrupted, "What? Cecil Pearce, the surveyor?" Eleanor was amazed. She hushed. Her mouth was wide open as well as her eyes. She looked at him sharply waiting for more information. So, he added, "We were close friends when we were at college. He was living at 29, Victor Street, here in Hungupville. Where's he now?" Tears won, and burst out of her eyes and ran warm on her cheeks. She was sobbing, unable to control herself, and so she ran out of the study and Mattie was following her crying. Gillian got back and said, "Joe's coming." When she didn't see Eleanor in her seat, she asked Fred, "Where's Eleanor?" Fred said, "She'd gone out crying since a minute." Gillian turned to get out but she changed her mind. She made half a turn and asked Mr. Fetters, "What was wrong with her?" "When I asked her about her husband Cecil Pearce, my old friend, she started weeping and left the room." Fred answered. Gillian nodded with a faint smile on her face and said, "It seems you haven't seen Cecil since a long time. He was killed in Asia a year ago." Fred felt sorry for Eleanor, for her child and for all the Pearces, but nobody had told him that sad news. On hearing the shocking news about Cecil, he himself was going to cry. Then, Mrs. Miese told him that the Pearces had moved to Lateburg when Mr. Pearce, Cecil's father, started a boutique there eight years ago. Upon his request, she gave him their address in Lateburg.

Two days later, on Monday at sunset, Fred was holding a bouquet of white and yellow daffodils in his hand and knocking at Eleanor's flat-door. When she opened the door, welcome tears poured from her eyes. She was surprised to see him with daffodils in his hand. When he was talking about Cecil and their adventures together and about Cecil's mother's homemade cakes and biscuits, Eleanor brought him some of those cakes and a glass of tea. She asked his permission for a minute to call somebody and got out of the room. She phoned up her mom-in-law; Cecil's mother, and asked her to come as quickly as possible. She had a friend whom she had known. He was Cecil's friend and his name was Fred Fetters; a mechanical engineer. Since Mrs. Pearce's house wasn't so far from Eleanor's, it took her about ten minutes to join them in Eleanor's house.

Diana Pearce was fifty-three years old, but she looked in her late thirties or at most in her early forties. She looked older than Eleanor, but she didn't look her mother. She was elegant, attractive and dressed in fashion. Her hair wasn't only silvered, but it was quite white long ago and so she dyed it weekly. She was a permanent customer of the beauty salons in Hungupville, then in Lateburg.

Diana was a real psychiatrist and choosy. She picked her words carefully to convey the exact meaning she targeted. She knew how to sit on a chair, in a seat or in a recliner sofa and how to cross her legs, to curl them under her or to join them and how to lean on something or to sit up. She knew how to look at things or at people; side look or in the face, shyly or sharp, gazing or glancing. She designed even her smile; faint or winsome, a broad, uncouth, outrageous, ironic or one in uncharacteristic display of emotions. Her laugh should be a sweet small, sexual, thrilling and roaring one or ironic. When she winked at people she chose the correct eye while smiling or laughing, meaningfully or meaninglessly. She had known how and when to screw her head round or to look at somebody over her shoulder. She had known well what to dress when and with whom or to whom.

When Eleanor rang her, she put on a hung purple tank, with a low plunging neckline, which was always ready to hand and her jeans which were small and tightened her thighs. They made her look sexier than any other woman her age. She always put them on to meet young people like Fred who thought her wearing a nightgown and jeans for the first while. He was popeyed with amazement but he smiled and dismissed the idea. Unless he had known her, he would have thought her a magazine girl.

In a minute, the old lady, Mrs. Pearce, was embracing Fred who was her son's friend and whom she is going to target as a boyfriend of hers. "Yes, they were close friends to each other." Eleanor decided. Then she determined to prepare them a light meal. Mrs. Pearce was very pleased when Eleanor brought the supper. It was exactly Cecil's favorite food which Fred liked very much. She remembered the least details. He reminded her of the pies, cakes and biscuits she provided them with when they were at college. Finally, she rose up, embraced him and said, "You're a nice guy, Fred. In spite of all those years, you didn't forget us." She said joyfully. Despite of the melancholic situation, the three of them felt happy. Then Fred said smiling teasingly, "I wish I could punch him on the face. He was jealous to tell me about his pretty wife." Eleanor, tortured between loss and hope, drew a breath and said softly, "What was broken couldn't be mended, but I'd remember him as long as I live." She loved Cecil to the last breath in his life, to the last beat of his heart, and she would love him to the last minute of her life. Nevertheless, that wouldn't prevent her from tempting another nice man who may ask to befriend her.

Mrs. Diana Pearce invited Fred alone for supper in her apartment next Thursday. "You remember the food I cook, don't you? Isn't it tasty?" She said in her affectionate and efficient way of speech. She nodded smiling and advised him not to have dinner on that day as the supper would be flavored and its smell would sharpen his appetite. Eleanor was listening carefully. Then she nodded with an ironic smile on her face and wondered, "Which supper would he have first?" Finally, Diana gave him her address and her phone number. He, too, gave them his address and his phone number.

Generally, women are patient and they have kind hearts. They cry for the least insult or pain. They also cry when they see people or animals suffer. They forgive and forget the wrong doings and the wrong doers and they can hide all secrets in the world if they want. Only one thing they can't hide; jealousy! They try to be patient and oppress their nerves, but they burst so soon when it comes to jealousy. When Mrs. Pearce invited Fred for supper, Eleanor felt jealous. The time she was alone, only a few minutes after Mrs. Pearce had gone out to her house, she called Fred to give her a lift next Thursday to have the supper with him in Mrs. Pearce's house. She said her mother-in-law called her apologizing because she forgot to invite her, and asked insistently to have supper with them next Thursday. Fred promised he would.

Next Thursday at seven pm, Eleanor, her child and Fred were ringing Diana's doorbell. They didn't phone her to tell her they were coming in a few minutes. She was in her lightest, shortest, smallest and the most transparent and sumptuous dress. She was almost naked with heavy makeup on her face. She opened the door to meet Eleanor face to face. She was shocked. Her face whitened then blackened. Her smile became a frown. Her joy became calamity. She signed to them to get in with her shaky hand and head, unable to speak. When she closed the door and turned back, she fainted. Eleanor, with a choking smile in her throat and in her mouth, held her in the arm and waist and made her lie in the nearest recliner. Then she turned and walked a few yards to the window and burst with laughter. Her tears fell and her breath was dropping. She had to sit on the nearest thing it happened to be. It was the dining table on which she supported herself. Fred recognized very well what was going in the inner mind of the two women, and so he smiled and nodded. Nevertheless he was unable to raise his eyes from Dianna. Fearing that Eleanor may notice him eyeballing her Mom, he felt how disgusting, shameful and low he would look; he would belittle himself. How he could love Eleanor and lust after her mom! Therefore, he rose up and walked to the window, too.

After the visit they gave to Diana Pearce, Fred and Eleanor got out friends. Although they called each other daily and met many times, he couldn't get into her bed then, nor had a word of love been mentioned from any of them to the other.

One week was left and Matt would take his finals. He hadn't been studying in the last few days. His mother was worried. She hesitated to talk to him or to his father. He might have studied when he was alone in his room; but he wasn't. His books were in their place. The Physics book was on the sofa days ago. It was dusty. The Biology book was on the shelf with another four books and two notebooks. The pencil needed to be sharpened and the pen dropped under the table days ago and it was still there. On the next day, she brought him a glass of milk and some biscuits on a tray. After half an hour, she returned to his room to take the tray and the empty glass. His head was still on his crossed arms on the table. The glass was still full and the biscuits were untouched. She asked him if he wanted anything from the kitchen, he only raised his head, shook it and returned again to the same position.

Four days passed and only three days were left. He wouldn't even scrape through his exams. How she would tell his father who would be shocked and perhaps clotted. They were talking last weekend about Matt and the university which they wanted him to go to. When Joseph asked her opinion, Gillian said, "Hungupville University, of course." He smiled scornfully and winked at her. Then he said boasting he had asked in the accounting section in the factory about the most famous universities in the world. They said Harvard in the U. S. A., Oxford and Cambridge in the U. K., Sorbonne in France in addition to Berlin University, Tokyo University and they added other important and famous universities all over the world. Gillian was thinking if Matt had failed his exams, there would be a scandal and what a scandal that would be! Joe would certainly fall dead. But she was helpless. Eventually, she decided to tell him. She said that Matt wasn't fine and he was moody. Perhaps he suffered something she didn't know. He was unable to study in the last few days. Joe was shocked. His face reddened, darkened and whitened. She implored him to be kind when he would talk to their only son. It was useless to be outraged in those critical days. Joe raised his head, thought a little and went straight to Matt's room. He knocked at the door and entered. Matt was still sitting on his chair with his head on his crossed arms on the table. Joe sat opposite to him laying his big arms on the table and initiated Matt, "I'm not going to waste time. I'm leaving you with your study in a minute. If you get 'A' in your finals, you'll get the car you want; the last model. Ok?" Gillian entered the room with two glasses of lemonade. Matt only raised his head, sat up on the chair, took the glass, had a sip and said, "Thanks Dad. Thanks Mom. Ok Dad, I will!" And he smiled at his parents. They both nodded and left the room.

Matt didn't know what to do. His Mom returned into his room. His PC was on, but silent dead. She nodded, sighed with pang and sorrow and left the room, closing the door behind her. A quarter of an hour later, his cellular phone rang. He only raised his head up and looked at it from his eye corner but he didn't take notice of the number. Then he returned to his previous position. Five minutes later, his mother returned in hot haste and called before she got into his room, "Matt, why didn't you answer the phone? It was Pamela Sompler. She implored me to tell you to answer the phone." Matt raised his head up and asked amazed, "Eh?" "Pamela Sompler will ring you up in a minute." He turned round and asked, "What? Pam? Pamela Sompler? Are you sure?" He didn't trust his ears. His mother nodded and smiled optimistically. He rose up quickly, kissed his mother on her cheek and rushed to the faucet and washed his face. He was drying it on a towel when his cellular phone rang again. He threw the towel on the bed and quickly answered, "Hello, Matt Miese 8877632."

Pam was really on the phone. "Hello Matt. This is Pam here." and she asked him whether he was fine. "I'm fine; quite fine. And you?" Matt said. "I'm fine, Matt. But there's a problem. My mother dropped seriously ill more than a week ago. I couldn't study and I don't think I'll be able to study in the next few days. Her case worsened. Only a week was left for the exam or a little less. It seems I haven't got any real chance to succeed." Matt interrupted, "Only three days!" "Oh! Three days only! I haven't a dog's chance of passing the exam. It would be scandal if I don't pass it. I'm worried, Matt. I don't know what I may do." She complained. Matt was very attentive when he was listening to Pam. He could repeat her words literally and with the same accent. "And how can I help you, Pam? It's my pleasure, but how?" Pam implored him with her soft voice, although in an agony, that he had only to show her his answer sheet. He can sit up leaning his back to his chair and raising his answer sheet as if he were reviewing his answers. She would be sitting behind him, looking at his paper and scanning the answers. "That's the whole story. It's simple, isn't it?" She said.

Matt had never fancied Pam seeking help from him. He would have dropped fainted if she had greeted him with only a couple of words in the school days: 'Good morning!' He smiled and his face was lighted with joy. He went back with his memory weeks ago when the principal met with them. He forgot her on the phone. "Hello, Matt! Are you still there?" "Look Pam, I'm sorry for your Mom, but I'm very happy to hear your voice. I'm the happiest creature in the universe. I . . ." "Matt!" Pam interrupted sweetly. "Ok, Pam. You'll pass with honors! Trust me! Just calm down!" Then Pam said laughing joyfully, "Are you serious, Matt?" "Certainly, I am. Best wishes to your Mom. Thanks for the call, Pam." "Thank you, Matt. Bye, bye." "Bye, bye, Pam." Pam always felt that Matt was an extremely intelligent handsome youth. She liked him really. When he spoke to the principal, his words were so natural and careless. She felt there was a shared connection between them. They ought to get out of the principal's office as friends, but their shyness, their integrity, their young ages, their inexperience and their contest in the classroom hindered that friendship.

It was too late to study. He would hardly scruple his finals. "What a scandal! What shame! It's the car, Pam, Dad, Mom! Oh, what would I do?" He murmured. Then he added, "Pam has her own cause. What shall I say to her? What shall I say to my teachers and my classmates? What would they think of me? A deceit or a liar! Maybe both! I'd be the scorn of the town for ages." He scratched his head and walked in his room aimlessly, kicking whatever his foot reached, unknowing what to do. Then he felt hungry. He hastened to the kitchen to have something to eat. He found much tasty and nutritive edible stuff, so he ate and ate and ate. What he ate on that meal was more than what he did in the whole last week. Then he returned to his room, closed the door behind him and lay on his bed. Soon, he was in a snooze.

He dreamed that Arnold, his classmate, and Pam were in love. Pam looked at him sharply and said, "Bastard! You promised to lend me a hand but you didn't keep your word. Arnold did even without a promise. What a kind and nice man he is!" She turned her face, slipped her arm in Arnold's and went away. He woke up and went straight to the bathroom. He had a quick shower and turned back to his room. He thought, "If I scrape my exams, there will be a scandal. If I don't there will be a scandal, too. If I cheat and they catch me red handed, there will be a scandal, but I'll succeed for sure if they don't, and I'll get the highest points then. Who knows? There is always a scandal in all cases. The third possibility isn't certain, but success is possible." He repeated, "If I weren't caught red handed!" He smiled thoughtfully. He would cheat!

He dressed and went straight to the nearest bookstore. He bought two rolls of white paper, one inch wide and twenty yards long each. He also bought a pair of small scissors and turned back home. He got into his room, closed the door behind him and locked it. He sat at his table to summarize and take notes. He was going to write on scraps of that roll of paper, but he thought a little. He was at loss: remorse, immorality and illegality. On the other hand, he would lose Pam, his dream. He would lose the car his father promised to buy him. He would lose his pocket money, fivefold. Finally he made his mind. No way! He should cheat! He hastily scrawled a lot of important notes on many long scraps of paper.

The start was with the Biology book. He took notes and summarized the first three lessons of chapter one on a side of about one-yard scrap. He did the same with the next three lessons of chapter two on the second side of the same scrap. He twisted it and put it in the right pocket of his pants. He put the second scrap which was about a yard and a quarter in the left pocket. Then he put the third scrap in the back right-pocket, and the fourth in the back-left one. There were thirty-three lessons; eleven chapters, in the Biology book. So, he needed six pockets. Where would he put the fifth and the sixth straps? He opened his closet and took his woolen coat out. The coat's pockets were four. That was good. He put the last two scraps in two coat pockets. It took him six hours to finish the Biology book.

He gave himself a break to have a soft drink. Then he lay on his bed and thought, "What would I say if I were asked about the woolen coat in that hot summer's day?" He would allege he was ill and he had a bad fever. They would believe him, not only because he was unexpected to lie, but also because he would be worried and terrified and so his face would be pale.

After that short break, he did the same with the Physics book. The first six lessons were summarized on the two sides of a scrap of paper and he put it in the right pocket, and so on. Then it was the Chemistry book, then the History book followed by the English Grammar book which was the last. He needed the last two days with their nights to have his pockets stuffed with that efficient scientific weapon.

In the morning, he put on his ordinary summer clothes and the woolen coat over them. As it was very hot, he was sweating heavily. So, he had to buy a large bottle of mineral water to compensate the lost liquid off his body.

In the examination room, he sat on his assigned chair in front of Pam. Neither she looked at him, nor did he. Any way, he didn't think of her at that moment. He was busy minded in his stuffed pockets. There were only twelve students in the room with one proctor to look over them. He couldn't cheat as Mr. Candy, the proctor, was watching them with eagle's eyes. The examination started at nine sharp in the morning. At nine twenty, someone was calling Mr. Candy aloud to hurry out and answer the phone. It was emergent. He ran to the opposite room, twenty yards away, leaving the students alone; without a proctor to supervise them. It was the golden chance for Matt. He got the scraps one by one out of his pockets and answered all the questions of all the subjects on the assigned answer sheets. Matt was writing silently in hot haste as if his hand were a machine. It took him around fifteen minutes to finish. When Mr. Candy returned to the room of the examinees, Matthew Miese handed him the answer sheets. The proctor was amazed and curious that he started checking the answers on Matt's sheets. Matt was flying when he was leaving the school. He neither looked for the chauffeur, nor did he look for the car. He took a taxi and went straight to his home.

At home, he was singing and dancing joyfully. "Hey Mom, Dad, where're you?" His Mom was in the front garden when she glimpsed him coming back from the examination and so she hurried into the house. She told him that his father hadn't come back yet. Then she asked him about his exam whether he could answer well. He said, "Dad promised me a new car and my pocket money will be fivefold if I get 'A' only. What will he do for me if I get 'A+', the maximum point?" His mother's face shone up. "It seems you did well in the exam." She said kiddingly and a big mocking smile appeared on her face. Then she asked him, "What did you do with this woolen coat on this hot summer's day?" She extended her hand and touched a pocket of the coat. He backed terrified, gave her a side look and went fast into his room. He closed the door behind him and took off the woolen coat. He was undressing when his cellular phone rang. It was Pam and so he answered the phone speedily, "Matt Miese, hello Pam." "Thank you, Matt. You're really great. Unless you put those scraps on your chair, I couldn't answer any question." Matt couldn't trust his ears. He repeated, "The scraps on the chair?" Pam asserted, "Yes, I took them. Thanks Matt. Bye!" She hung up. Matt fell down on the sofa behind him in his room. Then he checked his woolen-coat pockets. They were empty!

When the three-car patrol came to arrest Cap Simon Limonnes more than three decades ago, he wasn't at home. There was a clash with machine guns between the guards at the gate of his house and the patrol. Then his family; his wife and his two children, in addition to the three guards were killed in hand grenade explosions. Cap Limonnes could flee and cross the border to West Afasinamea safe. Later, as he was aware of the oppressing economic conditions of the country, he didn't accept their offer to be a political refugee. In a week, he flew to Nectarland. He worked as a security consultant of the same shopping mall where Mrs. Rockney was appointed later as a sales manager. He got married and had Edward from his second wife. Mr. Limonnes and Mrs. Rockney acquainted each other. With his new family, he paid the Rockmeys visits on the New Year, the Easter, May-Day and Christmas. By and by, he became a friend of Mr. Hans Rockney. When the fire in the shopping mall broke out and Mrs. Rockney passed away, he became the closest friend of Mr. Rockney who invited him to spend the weekends with him in the Grand House.

On the same day of the accident; on the Second of May, Jocelyn made her mind with determination not to turn back to Robert Dang or to the Miese's rooms. She decided it was time to move on to better pastures. Although she had no illusions about her ability, she disliked the way of life she was living; it was unbearable for her. She would desert it even if she were to panhandle. She knew well that she couldn't get more than servicing, waitressing or paddling anything as a job. That was her ability and her qualification.

As she was full of hope for the future which would never be worse than the present, and there would be a great opportunity to live a better life, she decided to immigrate to Nectarland where none knew her. She had to take life as it came. She asked Robert the fifty dollars he got from Joseph last night. Per usual, he rejected her request at the beginning, but she finally got it. As she had a very limited budget, she gathered information about cheap places to stay; youth hostels and BBs in addition to the cheapest methods of travelling in Nectarland. At the station in Hunupville, she got onboard the first train which was leaving for the capital.

On the train she dozed and dreamed that she was an easy prey to a new pimp who took advantage of her sordid poverty aiming at making her a call girl. She woke up terrified with the intent to atone her previous unforgettable mistakes. She took a solemn pledge that she would never demean herself again. She wanted to purge all those unhappy memories from her mind; from childhood up to that moment. She would be trustworthy, respectable, honest and dignified as far as she could. She had an invincible belief in that honesty is the best policy to live by. Over and above, she should be more cautious especially of men.

She managed to get an entry visa, booked a plane ticket and left for Nectarland. When she landed in one of Nectarland airports, she headed to a toy store at the airport and for five dollars, she bought a Pocket Combat Pistol which looked like a real one. Then she went to the cafeteria in search for a job; not for a light meal. "I don't know what the future will bring, but it can't be as painful or dissatisfying as the past." She murmured and two tears rolled down her cheeks. Then she sighed. She was changing to the better.

The easiest and the most available jobs, for the unskilled jobseekers, were always the menial ones; waitressing, housekeeping and, as she was taking care of her mother, she was experienced in elderly caretaking. She applied for a waitressing job in the cafeteria. As they had a vacancy, she was going to be interviewed at once.

A young man was having a light meal in the cafeteria and listening to her conversation with the chief server. He contemplated her from toe to head. She had respectable clothes; jeans and a long-sleeved shirt. He was in a dark blue suit with a necktie. He looked one of the elite. Then he called her and asked whether waitressing was her job. She crossed and said angrily, "It isn't your own business!" The man smiled and his hand reached into the inner pocket of his jacket and showed her his ID. He was a lawyer. Her face lit up with surprise and delight and she apologized. Then she said she was a teacher but she faced some trouble in her job and she resigned. She was a jobless new-comer and she had to work to support herself and to afford her necessities in her new homeland. He invited her to sit at the same table with him and ordered her a meal. Then he offered her to be a caretaker of his old father. She could work for a nice salary, accommodation, clothing and three meals a day free. She asked him if he were serious. He said his father was an octogenarian and he was living alone in his big house, fifty miles away from the city. He was unable to take care of him because he had to oversee his work for long hours a day. His father wasn't ill, but he needed laundry, cooking and serving at the same time. She can stay there with her partner or her husband. She told him she was alone. Then he said, "Well, you can go to the interview. I offer you one and a half of the salary they'll offer you." She nodded and went to the interview room. They offered her twelve hundred dollars a month and one free meal a day. Transportation and accommodation should be her responsibility. She apologized that she couldn't accept such a salary.

The man; the lawyer, had an idea about waitressing salaries. When she returned, he asked her about their offer. She said the truth. When Mr. Rockney said that giving care was a hard job and caretakers needed to manage their time; take care of the elderly, do household jobs and socialize, Jocelyn said that her mother was paralyzed and she alone took care of her for years. She was experienced in looking after the elderly and she knew well that caregivers needed to be patient. "Then we had it out. You'll accompany me to my father's house. He'll be very happy and you'll never repent. Deal?" Jocelyn nodded.

He drove to his father's. On their way to the Grand House, as they used to call it, he asked her, "By the way Miss . . . Oh I forgot to introduce myself. I'm Ralph Rockney." "Jocelyn Cherries, from Hungupville, West Afasinamea." She introduced herself. "By the way Miss Cherries, can you drive? Have you got any idea about security and first aid?" Jocelyn nodded and said, "Yes, of course. I won't disappoint you."

Jocelyn needed to gather her thoughts. She leaned her head on the passenger door and thought long of the past. She repented all those days she spent between the arms of men for one-night stay and she was near to tears. It was a kindness from a wise lawyer to offer her the job. When Mr. Rockney saw her preoccupied all the time she was sitting beside him, he wanted to socialize her, "You'll find my father an agreeable guy and his stories are funny. He doesn't stop reading books in the morning and tells you what he read in the evening, but he sleeps early. He's a sound sleeper and he sleeps well to the morning. Let him have his sleep out. Nevertheless, I bet you'll love him. But never fall in love with him! I warn you! (Laughing.) He's still in love with Mom although she passed away fifteen years ago." He said and burst with laughter. Jocelyn laughed, too.

When they got into the house, Ralph asked her to fill in a form he had in his hand. The house was two-storied, so vast and looked luxurious. It was set in a splendid landscape of gently-sloping green hills and it centered a one-acre orchard with drives leading to the outer gate and round the house. It had the most spectacular views imaginable. Nevertheless, it looked sadly neglected. The garden, too, was in a state of total neglect but as she had a burning ambition to succeed in her new homeland, she managed to get it together with the Grand House neat and tidy in less than two weeks. The old man handed her a bundle of keys, a cellular phone and a gun. She took the keys and the phone but she apologized for the gun. She headed to her bag and plucked her toy gun. When Mr. Hans Rockney saw it, he curved his eyebrows and said "Wonderful!" But he didn't try to examine it; he didn't touch it. Jocelyn smiled faintly but ironically.

Mr. Hans Rockney's mother was a Swede and his father was from Loraine, a boundary area between France and Germany. In his childhood and adolescence, he befriended French and German boys of his contemporaries. When he went to the university, he was specialized in Physics and he had been graduated only a few months before The Second Great War broke out. Regardless of his loyalty, his belief and his will, the German army called him for the draft. After three-month training, he was appointed in the military industries; an explosive factory. With his team, they developed the destructive weapons of the German army. Two things he disliked; military and politics with its pacts and parties. Aside from the training period, he had never carried any kind of arms. Nevertheless, he was promoted to Captain in the army at the end of the war.

H. Rockney was a polyglot that he could speak many languages. In the post war era, he went to Sweden in search for his mother. Unfortunately, he found out that she passed away four years ago. Then he travelled to the Balkans. He liked the climate, the resorts and the seashore and so he stayed there. He married and his wife was loyal and trustworthy. They were in love with each other. His son Ralph was born there; in the Balkans. As his wife was convinced of his opinions; Humanitarianism, she became a Human-Right activist. Since she was one of their opponents, politicians in office in the Balkans obliged her to resign. The income from the scientific-tool store which Hans started years ago couldn't afford their necessities especially when their son Ralph came to life. Consequently, they emigrated to Nectarland and lived in the capital more than fifteen years. Mr. Rockney worked as a consultant in a scientific-tool factory. When he received his first salary, he laughed and said that was equal to a Brigadier General's salary. His intimate friends laughed and nicknamed him BG!

Mrs. Rockney was employed in the sales department in a shopping mall. When a big fire broke out and the whole mall building was burning, tens of people perished and the possessions were heavily damaged. Unfortunately, Mrs. Rockney was among the victims. Later, the Rockneys received half a million dollars insurance. They bought the Grand House for that money more than ten years ago when Ralph was granted his Degree in Law.

Hans's love to his wife was a fact. Tears fell from his eyes whenever he talked about her. Sometimes, he roared with laughter and his eyes were filled with tears. The unforgettable joke he used to tell about her was that she was an indefatigable campaigner for civil liberties. She immigrated to that country to struggle against the human rights' violation but she found that the rights she aspired didn't reach the level of those in her new home land; human rights and freedoms were inviolable in Nectarland. Any way, he had to manage on his own for more than ten years; since his wife passed away.

Jocelyn was a new woman and Mr. Rockney was very happy with her. She was a ray of sunshine for him. She made her mind to be straight, respectable trustworthy and not to cheat, deceive or lie to anyone or to plot against anyone. Amazingly, her determination was constant. She, too, was glad as she felt safe and secure. The old man and his son were generous with her and they treated her well. She proved she wasn't intrinsically bad.

Three men rang the gate bell and Mr. Rockney answered by the intercom. "Mr. Rockney, we're sorry for this intrusion, but we want to speak to you urgently, only for a few minutes, please." One of them said. Mr. Rockney walked to the outer gate and opened it. "Please, come in." He led the three men into the sitting room inside the house. "Please feel free." He said. Then he turned his head to the door and called aloud, "Jocelyn!" Jocelyn came at once and said, "Yes, Mr. Rockney." He pointed at the three men and said, "These men are our guests and you're hospitable!" Jocelyn smiled and said, "What would you like to drink, gentlemen?" "Any fizzy drink, please." Jocelyn turned and left the room. "How can I help you?" Hans Rockney said. "Mr. Rockney, our friends abroad are oppressed. They want to start a factory for explosives and they seek your help." One of them said. "Gentlemen, I was an officer in The Great War but I have never shot any living thing, not only human beings. I'm humanitarian and a pacifist! I may take part in building canned-food factories for an example. I aspire to see people happier and more peaceful, but building a factory for explosives isn't humane from my view point." "But those people, our friends, are oppressed." The man asserted. "There are other peaceful means to get their rights in full." Mr. Rockney said. "Mr. Rockney, I'm authorized to offer you one hundred thousand dollars as a monthly salary." Another one of them said enthusiastically.

"Gentlemen, I'm eighty-eight and I'm a pensioner. I have my own house and my own car. What would I do with that money you offer? What you offer is a bribe; it's the price of stinging remorse. It's neither a salary nor a donation. Nothing would tempt me to accept your offer. I do oppose bloodshed, fighting and killing. It's a principle. I'm sorry." Mr. Rockney said. Then he turned his face to the door and said aloud, "Jocelyn! The drink! Our guests are leaving." They all stood up stunned and left The Grand House.

Jocelyn usually went shopping at ten am, driving her pick-up truck along a narrow and skew road between orchards and vineyards. She always returned around noon. A group of people had been watching her since the first week of her arrival at the Grand House. They have scouted the house and they were aware of the alarm system. Jocelyn glimpsed them around. At first, she took them to be farm workers. Then she suspected them. She conveyed her suspicions to her employer Mr. Rockney who rang his son Ralph and told him to bring the two collies on their farm to the Grand House. As it was Friday, at a late hour in the afternoon, Ralph arrived with his wife Nancy and his two children; Lora and Patrick, seven and three years old respectively. They have the two dogs; Thunder and Star with them. The Rockneys were very happy to see the house very clean and well-taken care of. It was perfectly immaculate. The old man expressed his satisfaction with Jocelyn's work and her awareness.

Jocelyn played with the children. Then at sunset, she prepared a nice supper for the whole family. A nice smell of cooking permeated through the house. The two kids felt hungry as their appetites were sharpened, they peeped to the kitchen every couple of minutes to have their supper as soon as possible.

To be familiar with the dogs, Jocelyn gave them half a chicken each only to be able to touch them smoothly and to wipe their backs and their heads. Then she offered them two big pieces of meat as a reward. Later, whenever they felt her approaching, they rose up to their limbs and wagged with their tails to receive her and her donation. She adapted herself quickly to the new job.

The intruders hadn't taken the dogs in consideration when they returned to the Grand House to put a plan they had prepared into action. They were stunned to see the two collies free; roaming the orchard around the house. Therefore, they had to postpone their plan or to abandon it. For the alarm system, they were professionals; they had a good experience of what to do in such cases. Any way, they turned back empty-handed that night.

A few days later, the dogs barked insistently. Hans Rockney moved the curtain, which the sun had faded, a little and peeped out. Two of the intruders were running towards the front door of the house. They had opened the gate with a master key and crossed the front garden. A third had climbed up a tree under which the dogs were barking behind the house. Mr. Rockney went to the balcony to warn them: either they leave or he would call the police, but they hurried upstairs even before he was able to leave the balcony.

On her way to the town, Jocelyn glimpsed their truck among the trees. She suspected their intentions and so she made only a little shopping and turned back home as fast as possible. Their truck had been parked at the gate which was open wide. The dogs were still barking behind the house. She hurried to the hall of the ground floor where she heard shouts and loud noises coming from the upper floor and so she let her toy gun off. The sound was terrifying. The two men upstairs were stunned and the uproar hushed down. Then she shouted aloud, "Hey, you there! Either, you get downstairs and leave the house quietly and safe in a second or I'll call the police. Otherwise, you'll be plugged full of holes if you try any more aggression. Just climb down and get out. I give you my word!" She showed a lot of pluck in dealing with them. They climbed downstairs slowly. One of them told her that they were only talking to Mr. Rockney. They didn't intend to harm him or to steal anything. "Get out of here and never get back again!" Jocelyn said aloud. They hurried to the gate. When the dogs felt them in the front garden, they returned heading to the intruders, but Jocelyn pacified them. The third man, who had climbed up the tree, climbed down and jumped over the wall before the dogs were able to turn back to him. The three men jumped into their pick-up truck and drove away. When she heard the engine of their truck and she was sure they had left away, she hurried to the gate, locked and chained it.

Then she turned back quickly into the house and climbed up stairs jumping twos or threes at a time. When she got into her employer's bedroom, he was handcuffed and wrapped with a carpet under his bed. She freed and hugged him. He was in a state near the death. They both cried. He was bleeding. There was a serious wound on his forehead and another on his back. He would certainly die if a doctor didn't see him so soon. She called the ambulance and rang his son Ralph. She got with him into the ambulance and hurried to the emergency room in the nearest hospital where he stayed three days during which Jocelyn didn't part him; day or night. When he was well and his face regained color, she drove him back to the Grand House.

Mr. Rockney felt depressed in the following few days, but soon he perked up when his friend; Simon Limonnes with his son Edward, who was in his thirties then, arrived at The Grand House. As a friend, Simon was always able to get Mr. Rockney attentive by not talking about Mrs. Rockney whom Hans was trying hard to forget. Simon had never talked about her. His aim was to make him laugh and to forget her. He always asked him to dress well and to go somewhere to have dinner or supper with him or with any other nice company outdoor.

When Jocelyn brought the fruit juice to Mr. Rockney and to his guests Simon Limonnes and his son Edward, the latter asked her whether she was an Afasinamean. Mr. Rockney laughed and said, "I forgot to tell you that Jocelyn descended from an East Afasinamean family but she lived in the West." Then he added, "How did you know?" Simon said they heard her talking to someone in the Afasinamean language. "Yes, I was born and brought up in West Afasinamea but my parents came from the East." Jocelyn said smiling. "Sit down, Jocelyn. Simon's your fellow citizen; formerly and currently." Mr. Rockney said laughing.

Late in the afternoon, Mr. Rockney gave directions to Jocelyn to show Edward Limonnes the whole orchard, to feed the dogs and to pluck some ripe fruit. The Limonnes were going to spend the night in the Grand House. Then he jerked with his hand gesturing to them to go together to the orchard. Both were very happy. Then Mr. Rockney and Simon Limonnes drew the curtain a little and peeped at Jocelyn and Edward. They were extremely happy to see the young couple smiling, laughing and talking amusingly and enjoyably.

The intruders had never been hopeless as they were with Mr. Rockney. They decided to talk to Jocelyn and so one of them came abreast of her and signaled her to stop when she was driving along the narrow road between the orchards and the vineyards on her way to the market. She closed the driver window quickly and withdrew her toy gun from a pocket in the tableau and aimed at the man, who was close to the driver door of her pick-up truck, threatening him to explode his head if he moved one more inch forward. The man stopped and signed to her to calm down. He wanted to talk to her not to harm her. Therefore, she opened the window a slit and listened to him. He tried to share her in their plot offering her a hundred thousand dollars. She tightened her lips disapprovingly, closed the window and warned him to get out of her way. The man turned back frustrated and she drove on. She rang Mr. Rockney and told him what had happened. He told her to go to the police who took strict precautions to protect Jocelyn, Mr. Rockney and the Grand House. Some people were a serious threat to her life and to Mr. Rockney's.

XXII

Weeks ago, Eleanor told Louisa about the time she had spent in the Mieses' country house on May-Day vacation. Louisa was very happy to hear the good news that Eleanor had changed her mind and kissed her on her cheeks, winked at her and said laughing, "Your cuts recover quickly and well!" Then she told Eleanor that she could send Mattie to her house any time she had a date. The two kids; Louisa's and Mattie, would spend a nice time together.

On his way out from Mrs. Diana's house, Fred Fetters invited her and Eleanor to have dinner at a sea shore restaurant, twelve miles from Lateburg, next Sunday. After dinner, they would go to the movies at four pm. Then they would have a rest at his house and have a quick-meal supper. After that, they would spend some time in one of the café houses at the sea shore or they would go to a night club to dance. Diana apologized for the dance as they were only three; not four and that Mattie wouldn't be allowed to admit any night club. They all agreed.

On their way to Eleanor's place, Eleanor told Fred she liked to see that sea-shore restaurant and to go to the night club on Friday evening; the next day. She hadn't gone to any club since one and a half years. Fred burst with laughter and said, "I have the same idea! If you had waited only one second, I'd have invited you." On Friday when the school finished, Louisa took Mattie with her to her house and Eleanor went to the beauty salon.

On their way to the sea shore, Fred was driving so slowly. Eleanor asked him teasingly whether there was a problem in his car, he smiled and said, "I won't see or hear anything or (looking in her eyes) anyone more attractive than what I can hear and see! Why should I drive fast?" Eleanor's face reddened and she smiled shyly and thanked him. Fred raised his eyebrows, smiled faintly and said to himself, "A successful start!"

When they were together on the same boat and on the islet of daffodils, tulips and jasmine, Eleanor said to herself, "I've found the good man!" Fred, too, said to himself, "I've been waiting long for a woman like you! Now I'm sure I'm lucky!" Later, both wondered silently how and when they would meet. More than her name, Fred knew nothing about her, and she had only known he was an engineer in Miese's Factory. Eleanor sat on a bench and watched two snipe battling for a little chub in shallow water where a rivulet met the sea. The fish was moving joyfully under the golden rays of the evening sun. Fred was observing her closely. Then he said teasingly, "What do you think of those two battling snipe? Are they males or females?" She burst with laughter and dropped her head shyly. Then she said, "You first!" Fred bit his finger nail thoughtfully and said, "Well, I'll tell you the snipe sex and you'll tell me the chub sex. Deal?" "No. Not deal." She said sweetly. "I'll tell you the snipe's sex and you'll tell me the fish sex. It's fair!" "Okay. Fire away!" He accepted. "The snipe are females!" She said laughing. "Wonderful! How did you know?" Fred asked. "Because the fish is a male!" She said and burst with laughter. Fred, too, laughed until he lay down on his back on the sand breathless. When he had himself, he asked her permission for one more question; only one! "What would they do if the fish were fat and adult?" Eleanor laughed shyly and hurried to him and hid her face on his chest. He held her chin with his hand, raised her head, kissed her on her nose tip and returned her head to its place on his chest wiping her smooth and long hair. She heard his heart beats. A moment later, she raised her head, hugged and kissed him a long, long one. Abruptly, an artillery shell past whistling over their heads and splashed the sea water. The whole place vibrated when it exploded. Both of Eleanor and Fred were shocked and terrified. They hurried to the car breathless and turned back to Lateburg.

Both of Eleanor and Fred loved each other but they were courting for a year before they finally married. The two felt so happy to share one another's life.

XXIII

On the First of May, there was a coup in East Afasinamea. The democratic civilian government was thrown over and a new military one ruled the country. Since the borders, as well as the minorities, had always been a bone of contention between the two Afasinameas, and in the absence of a democratic government in the East, there were bombing, shelling and air-raiding across the border against each other. Around the mid of July, East Afasinamea shelled and their planes bombed heavily military and nonmilitary targets in West Afasinamea. Innocent blood was split and many block buildings and whole factories were wiped out. The Miese's Butter, Cheese & Cream Factory in Hungupville was one of them. It was completely destroyed. As Mr. Miese didn't believe in insurance, in addition to the one million dollar cash he had given as donation to the Four Us charities and the money he paid to repair the broken machines last May, he was unable to restore his factory nor could he buy a new one. As the gross national product drastically dropped down in the two Afasinameas and the budget had been pared to the bone, the Western government was unable to compensate those who lost their houses, factories, workshops or their work in general as a result to the non-stop and undeclared war between the two Afasinameas. Peace and more funds were required to invigorate the country's industry and its economy in general but both were missing. No way! The economy was in tailspin. The industry faced an uncertain future and the new tax laws affected most people.

Gillian suggested immigrating to Nectarland. With the price of their estates in West Afasinamea, they would be able to start a new factory or a new business there. Joseph hesitated at first. When Gillian told him that he could talk to the engineer; Mr. Fred Fetters, he instantly phoned him up. Fred roared with laughter and told him that he himself was thinking to leave for Nectarland. If they decided to immigrate to Nectarland or to any other country they could email him. Anyway, they could help each other and start a new work together there.

Many businesses had closed down because of the recession that resulted from the undeclared war between the two Afasinameas. With the base on the North Mountain, the West Afasinameans, as well as the Easterners, had the fears that the conflict might be internationalized although the base-force purpose would never exceed the logistic support. The country; West Afasinamea, was going to rack and ruin and a change of government only was of no use. And so the Mieses, as well as a lot of industrialists, investors and graduates decided to leave their homeland where they were born and lived. They had the determination to immigrate to Nectarland. Therefore, they sold their estates and everything they owned, booked the plane tickets and headed to the airport. By a quirk of fate, at the departure hall, they were surprised to find Christina and Michael sitting in a recliner. "Hello, what're you doing here?" Gillian initiated. They both stood up and received them with open arms. "As we're graduates and qualified, we're immigrating to Nectarland in search for peace and happiness, and you?" Christina said. "We're immigrating, too, but as investors!" "Yes, Nectarland receives qualified immigrants, investors and refugees on humanitarian grounds." Michael concluded nodding. "It's very strange. The Mieses are very rich. Why are they immigrating?" Christina whispered in Michael's ear. "Yes, they're rich, but that doesn't necessarily mean they're safe or happy. All of us are in search for safety, security and happiness."

When the Mieses, Michael and Christina heard the announcement for the plane, they all cried and sang a song of great poignancy and beauty in the departure hall at the airport.

The Mieses, as well as some of their friends and their acquaintances, were lucky to have a refuge in Nectarland. Others, of East Afasinamea, crossed the borders to the nearest neighbouring states only to survive. They were terrified and chased by hunger, diseases, unemployment, and overall the IGA men.

XXIV

In six months, the old man, Hans Rockney, was sure of Jocelyn's loyalty, honesty, bravery and faithfulness. So were his son and his family. They were touched by Jocelyn's faithfulness. They had never felt that Jocelyn was a housekeeper or a caretaker. They considered her the sixth member of the Rockney family. The old man wanted to change his will, but his son the lawyer inclined to postpone it until a more suitable time. When Jocelyn completed the eleventh month in her job and she was the best example of a wonderful caretaker, house keeper and a nurse when the old man was seriously ill, her employer had the determination to change his will. His son didn't find any more excuses to delay his father's intent and so he had to give up. They both prepared it and the old man reviewed it more than once before he finally signed it. The new act which was added to the old man's will was that Jocelyn should choose between the house in addition to her salary which should be monthly as long as she was alive or three quarters of a million dollars cash after his death. His will should be top confidential. They both went to the law court to sign it and to leave a copy there. Since none of the Rockneys was at home, Jocelyn didn't need to go shopping that day; she had to stay at home until her employer's return.

Hans Rockney's health deteriorated dramatically and rapidly and he passed away in a month. Jocelyn felt so sad for his death. She cried and rivers of tears rolled down her cheeks. On the eighth day when the dead man's will was announced, she consulted the lawyer for the right choice. He apologized and told her he couldn't give her any advice as he himself was an heir. She could consult another lawyer. And so she went to the bank where the money was deposited and asked the manager his advice. He called the director of investment to ask him his advice, "If you were an heir, which one would you choose; the house and what follows or the cash money?" Jocelyn asked him.

Since she'd set her heart on getting a degree, she got out of the bank and went straight to the registrar in the nearest university to be enrolled in the next term. She did well at the university as she had the intent and the determination to get her BA with honors. She strongly believed in the saying "Where there's a will, there's a way!"

Finally, Jocelyn made the good decision of her own accord. She chose the house and the salary. When property was made over to her and she got the ownership documentation of the Grand House, she cried. Jocelyn's story was a true rags-to-riches one.

She thought long of her past and present situations. If she had known what the future had held for her, she would have never involved in any illegal or immoral activities; she would have never demeaned herself. That lawyer was a fairy godmother. He could have advertised an elderly care job and he would have received hundreds of applications without her knowledge. Had she traveled from her mother homeland to her new home—land to get that job by chance? She wondered.